HEARTS OF THE WEST

His Fearless Heart

The Bull Rider's Baby Surprise

By Jennifer Lewis

1

Lucy could feel heads turn and eyes dart toward her as she walked into the dining room of the Singing Pines Ranch. The new dress her friend had talked her into buying was black and hugged her curves snugly, revealing far more of her figure than she would normally dare. As she moved toward the buffet, two good-looking young men at a nearby table ceased their conversation to stare at her.

She felt a hot flush of embarrassment rise up from her low cut cleavage. What was she thinking? She'd always preferred to blend into the background. She wasn't beautiful, even with all the unfamiliar makeup she'd applied tonight. The other diners were probably laughing at her for trying to turn the proverbial sow's ear into a silk purse.

She picked up a plate at the buffet and helped herself to some pasta salad and a piece of chicken.

"You should try the lobster, it's fresh." A low voice in her ear made her turn to see one of the men had moved up behind her.

"Really?" She avoided looking at him as she helped herself to a menacing red claw. The lobster probably wasn't the only thing that was fresh.

"How long are you here for?"

Lucy turned and had to look up since he was tall and stood so close. She fought a powerful urge to blush because he was so damned gorgeous—jade green eyes sparkling with mischief, skin tanned and weathered by the sun, hair streaked with gold. A small scar bisected his left eyebrow.

She struggled to gather her thoughts into a coherent reply. "Four days. I arrived this morning."

"Are you dining with someone or would you like to join us? I'm sitting with my brother Jesse. He owns the place." He indicated the table, where the other man, also frighteningly handsome but with darker hair, raised a glass.

"I'm not here with anyone." Panic flooded her. She'd promised her best friend Val that she'd make an effort. If she had dinner with them, that would count, right? "I'd be happy to join you." Her heart started to pound at the prospect of having to make conversation with strangers, particularly such intimidatingly attractive strangers.

"I'm Bowie West, pleased to meet you." He held out his hand. Lucy transferred her plate to her left hand and shook it. His handshake was firm and warm, and he looked intently at her while he pressed her palm to his. Heat rushed up her arm and she felt herself growing flustered.

He led her to the table without stopping to get food for himself. Apparently he'd gotten up only to talk to her. Was her makeover that much of a transformation? Maybe she did look good.

Bowie pulled out a chair for her and she eased herself into it, hoping that none of the seams on her dress would pop.

"This is Jesse."

"My pleasure," said the other man, who had risen from his chair as she approached the table. "And what's your name?"

"Lucy, Lucy Neel," she realized she'd forgotten to introduce herself to Bowie.

"Champagne?" asked Bowie.

"Yes, thank you," managed Lucy. Bowie's tanned forearm flexed as he poured a glass for her. The two men were dressed like ordinary cowboys, in well-worn jeans and checkered shirts. She didn't think she'd ever seen cowboys drink champagne before.

"Jesse, do you want anything else to eat?"

"No thanks, I'm okay. Maybe I'll have some dessert in a while but I can get it myself."

"Jesse pulled a groin muscle getting bucked off a bull a couple of days ago. He's recuperating," said Bowie.

"Why were you riding a bull?" asked Lucy, thinking that she should make some effort in the conversation.

"That's a good question," said Jesse, with a laugh.

"Because it's what we do," said Bowie. "We're both professional bull riders."

"Speak for yourself," said Jesse, dark eyes twinkling. "I'm retired. Mostly I train horses these days, but Bowie convinced me to breed a couple of bucking bulls here at the ranch and I was fool enough to get on one. This particular bull demonstrated impressive talent."

"I want to try him," said Bowie, with a wink at Lucy.

"Be my guest." Jesse turned to Lucy. "We usually do a bull riding demo here after dinner, and Bowie's volunteered to stand in for me. Don't get too attached to him."

"I won't," she said quickly.

"Jesse won't admit I'm a better bull rider than him." Bowie cocked his chin with confidence. Then he looked at Lucy and she could see that even though his eyes were on her face, he was really looking lower, at the embarrassing expanse of cleavage revealed by her new black dress.

The look on his face showed that he liked what he saw. Lucy burned with embarrassment. It was encouraging that she looked good enough to attract the attention of such a handsome man, but she also felt forward, like she was putting her goods on display.

On the other hand, at twenty-seven years old and still a virgin, it was time she put her goods in the marketplace before any more dust gathered on them.

Lucy took a sip of her champagne and the bubbles tickled her nose. She hardly ever drank and she was sure it would go to her head, but maybe that was just the confidence booster she needed.

"How did you get into bull riding?" she asked.

"My mom said it's because I'm crazy." Bowie winked. "But I stopped hearing that when I started winning titles."

"Sounds like a lot of fun. Does it pay well?" Lucy bit her tongue as soon as she'd asked. It sounded so rude to ask him if he earned a lot of money. Bowie looked at her for a second then tilted his head.

"Not bad."

Jesse leaned forward. "He's being modest. It pays extremely well, especially when you're on top. This year Bowie intends to win the world finals, which comes with a million dollar bonus."

"Jesse knows this firsthand because he won it two years ago."

Lucy tried not to act too star struck. These handsome young men—flirting with her boldly enough to make her toes curl—were obviously two of the top bull riders in the country. "That's pretty cool. Though I'm glad my work mostly involves staying on an animal's back, not falling off it."

"What do you do for a living?" he asked.

Pride swelled in her chest. "I own a horse farm."

"No kidding?" He looked impressed. "Where is it?"

"About twenty-five miles east of here. I have twenty-three horses there right now. I board horses for clients, teach lessons, and buy and sell horses. It's all English riding, so it's a little different for the area."

Bowie nodded his head, appraising her yet again with those penetrating green eyes that did something strange to her insides. "So what are you doing here when you already live on a ranch?"

"I won the getaway weekend in a hunter pace competition."

"Excellent," said Jesse. "They asked me to donate a prize and I hoped it would go to someone who'd enjoy it."

Bowie leaned in. "So who's minding the store while you're away?"

"I have help." Poor Luis was probably exhausted trying to do all the work himself on top of his regular job, but he'd insisted that she go away and take the trip. He knew she couldn't afford to pay an additional person to help out.

"Well I'm glad you decided to hang your spurs here for the night," said Bowie. His green eyes glittered dangerously. He had a slightly piratical look to him. He wasn't wearing gold earrings and an eye patch but they wouldn't have been too out of place either.

She couldn't help smiling. "I rarely use spurs."

"You prefer more subtle methods of persuasion?"

Bowie leaned back in his chair and crossed his arms in front of him. His white-and-blue-checked shirt emphasized his dark tan and the rolled up sleeves revealed the muscles in his strong arms.

"Yes, even retraining if necessary. In fact, making hard horses sensitive again is one of the things I specialize in."

"You sound like a dangerous lady."

"Not dangerous, just patient and persistent."

"You're being pretty patient and persistent with that lobster claw, but it's not getting you too far. Do you want me to crack it open for you?"

Lucy blushed. She'd been trying unsuccessfully to reach her fork inside the claw for several minutes.

"Here." He took the claw off her plate, wrapped it in a napkin, and crushed it with a quick blow from his empty water glass. "Sometimes there's no substitute for brute force." He unwrapped the shattered claw and put it back on her plate.

"Thanks." She stabbed the newly liberated tender flesh with her fork. Somehow it seemed very intimate to have someone manhandle your lobster claw. The lobster was good though.

Jesse sat silently, with a slight smile on his face, leaning back in his chair as if watching a show. Lucy wasn't sure she was cut out to play a principal role in anyone's dinner theater. And she'd a feeling that this show might be an encore performance of a role that

Bowie played with some regularity.

And the way Bowie was looking at her, as if he'd like to crack open her shell and eat her all up, was doing something rather unsettling to her stomach.

Bowie's phone rang and he glanced at it, then put it back down. "Weird."

"What?" asked Jesse.

"Someone keeps calling me about a prize she thinks she won. I told her I have no idea what she's talking about, but she won't quit. I just blocked her."

They chatted about horses and bulls and the contests he'd entered already that year while they enjoyed dessert, then the men excused themselves to go get a bull ready for the demo.

"I'll be mortally offended if you don't come watch me," said Bowie with that characteristic sparkle.

"I'll be there." She stole a quick trip to the ladies' room, mostly to take a peek at herself in the mirror and see what Bowie West was looking at.

Not bad. In fact, she barely recognized herself. She could even see how a man would find her attractive. The cut of the dress made her look curvy rather than dumpy, which was how she would normally have described her figure. She'd been bullied in school for being fat and never felt confident about her body.

The makeup emphasized her features and made her look a little sultry. She'd let the hairdresser talk her into getting blonde highlights in her dark hair, and she'd to admit that they gave her a new look, flirtier and more eye-catching.

What was wrong with letting this other girl, the one with the blonde streaks in her hair and the low cut dress, have a little fun?

The champagne must have gone to her head

because she felt daring. Would Bowie seek her out after the demo? He'd be the star of the show and probably every girl in the place would mob around him.

She touched up her lipstick. *Don't be too cautious and blow it. Take a chance and have an adventure.* So far stepping out of her comfort zone was going pretty well and she might have an exciting tale or two to share with Val when she got back home.

She joined the people headed outside to watch the demo in the arena. Young live oaks ringed the arena, their branches twinkling with tiny white fairy lights in the gathering dusk. The whole ranch was beautifully decorated, with clay pots filled with flowers, perfectly swept and manicured paths, and neatly painted fencing.

Maybe her place would look like that if she'd a million dollars in prize money to spend on it. At least it was good for inspiration.

She found a spot to lean on the fence, and waited with growing anticipation as the arena lights snapped on and Jesse's warm voice boomed over the loud speakers.

"And now, ladies and gentlemen, let me present the star of the show and one of the hottest up-and-coming prospects for next season—Little Red Wagon." Lucy laughed, along with the others, who had been expecting him to say Bowie's name.

She peered into the gloom, where she could hear shuffling and breathing in the pen just beyond the arena lights. "Riding the Little Red Wagon today is a man that most of you know by name and reputation as the finest rider on the circuit—now that I've left it—my brother Bowie West."

The crowd cheered and Bowie exploded through the gate on the back of a chestnut-colored bull. Did they call bulls chestnut? Or was it different from horses? The bull heaved himself around, throwing his hind legs up in the air.

Lucy was half afraid to look at Bowie—who flew around in circles with the bull, one arm gripping the bull and the other high in the air. His straw cowboy hat flew off and she gasped.

If he lost his grip, he'd be tossed across the arena like a rag doll, and possibly smashed on the fence or trampled by the wildly spinning bull.

The crowed clapped out each of the eight seconds he'd to stay on the bull: one, two, three— Lucy wanted to cover her eyes and open them up when it was safely over, but she couldn't. Bowie was looking straight at her, those daring green eyes fixed right on hers.

2

Bowie stayed with Little Red Wagon as if he were glued to his broad back. His eyes left Lucy's as the bull charged across the arena, but he didn't lose his grip. Once the crowd had clapped to eight, the cheering intensified, and Bowie waved to the crowds before unwinding the rope from his hand and leaping clear of the bull with impressive athleticism.

Lucy let out an audible sigh of relief and realized she'd been holding her breath the whole time. Eight little seconds could be an eternity!

And Bowie had picked up his hat and was striding right toward her. She blinked as he put one hand on the fence and jumped right over it, then gasped as he landed only inches in front of her.

"Congratulations," she managed, though she was still barely breathing. She felt a goofy grin spread across her face.

"Why, thank you, ma'am." He swept his hat with his hand and bowed low. She giggled at the grandiose gesture.

"You deserve to win a million dollars for that ride."

"It's all in a day's work." Bowie grinned. "Though I've already told Jesse that bull is going to make him a lot of money. He's a talented animal."

Lucy laughed. "He's rather stunning. I'm glad you're riding him not fighting him like they do in Spain."

"Riding bulls is a lot more fun than killing them. Breeding them is pretty interesting, too. I plan to set up my own ranch soon, so I can get serious about it."

A band had set up on a small stage over to one side of the dining room, which opened to the outdoors. As the musicians struck up a tune, couples moved across the floor to dance. It was a slow, sexy number with a Latin influence.

"Would you like to dance?" asked Bowie.

"Uh, I don't really know how to dance." Apparently even golden highlights didn't give her the self-confidence to try and strut her stuff on a dance floor.

"You don't need skills to dance a slow dance." Bowie took her hand, "Come on." He took her hand, which thrilled her, and led her under the twinkling lights in the trees toward the softly lit dance floor.

Once they were among the dancers, Bowie placed his other hand on her waist and stepped toward her. Her skin hummed where he touched her, and her belly shimmered as he drew close. She could almost feel sparks flying in the air between them.

Lucy remembered the champagne in her veins and tried to let her body flow with his as he guided her in the dance. They made small steps together, Bowie's chest only a few inches from hers. Excitement sizzled through her as she swayed gently to the rhythm of the music, with Bowie's hand resting on her hip.

An evening breeze, scented with mesquite from the grill, cooled her skin. Over Bowie's shoulder she could see the last glow of pink sun setting behind the wooded hills. His chiseled chin was at eye level and she decided that from now on she only liked men with a fine layer of sexy stubble, just like Bowie.

"You're a liar." His gruff words made her look up. "And a good dancer,"

"I give the champagne full credit." *And you.* Bowie brought out something inside her that she didn't even know was there.

Those teasing green eyes grazed over her with admiration, making her face heat and her skin tingle. With Bowie she felt like a goddess. There were some very beautiful women here, but he'd chosen her from among them. He'd seen her and decided that she was the one he wanted to dine with, to dance with...and maybe even to take back to his room.

If he asked her, would she dare?

She enjoyed the weight of his hand on her hip, the warmth of it though the thin fabric of her dress. Lucy began to wish that he would pull her a little closer. Heat rose between their bodies as they moved and gyrated together.

As if he'd read her mind, Bowie moved toward her, his fingers splayed and his palm resting on her bare back. Only about an inch of space separated her body and his. That inch of space was getting very warm. She didn't dare look up at him but she sensed his eyes upon her, looking at her, drinking her in as he danced.

"You are the most beautiful woman here tonight."

"Am I?" She didn't really believe him. As soon as the words left her mouth she regretted them. She sounded as though she were fishing for further compliments.

"Without a doubt. Would you like to take a walk outside?"

"Yes." Lucy was a little sad that Bowie wouldn't be holding her body so close any longer. Then again, she wasn't sure how much more close contact she could take before she would lose her wits altogether.

She probably hadn't danced with a man since she let Joey Reid take her to the junior prom all those years ago. And he'd just been a nice geeky guy who lived down the street, not a lithe and sexy athlete with a devilish grin.

Bowie led her through the dancing couples and out onto the veranda. The September evening air was cooling a little—just perfect. A big silver moon hung huge and heavy over the horizon, bathing the land in an otherworldly glow.

Bowie led her to a hanging swing bench and held it while she seated herself on it. So far so good, the dress hadn't burst apart yet. The fabric was a bit stretchy so that probably helped.

Bowie settled himself beside her on the bench and put his arm around her shoulder. She stiffened.

Maybe she looked like an easy mark. Men weren't exactly falling over each other rushing to be by her side. He probably thought he was doing her a big favor by bringing her out here and placing his arm on her shoulders.

Stop it, Lucy! Don't ruin this magic moment by worrying about what he is and isn't thinking. What did she know, anyway? She'd just spent wasted years in a long-distance "relationship" with a man who turned out to be gay.

Go with the flow, relax, and enjoy whatever happens.

"Are you going on the trail ride tomorrow?" he

asked.

"The overnight camp out? Yes, I'm looking forward to it. Are you?"

"If you're going, definitely. So tomorrow night we'll be sleeping out under the stars together." He said it with a hint of suggestion, but Lucy knew that since they would be part of a group and would have no privacy, hinting was as far as he would get. Still, it was a nice idea. She liked the idea of seeing his handsome face sleeping, the flickering reflected firelight dancing across his cheekbones.

"I don't think I've ever slept outdoors before," she said. "I visited a dude ranch with my parents once. They hated it and insisted on skipping the evening ride and sleeping in the cabins overnight. I was so mad! I wanted to soak up every second of the experience. That trip is when I started dreaming about having my own ranch."

"How long ago was that?"

"A long time, probably almost ten years."

"I guess it made a big impression on you."

"It did. We hardly ever went anywhere. My dad was a pastor and busy with his flock all the time. We actually went there for some kind of Bible study retreat. I had such a good time that I knew I wanted to live like that for the rest of my life."

"And now you do."

She laughed. "Not exactly. My day to day life is more about shoveling manure and measuring scoops of pelleted feed, not galloping through the open country."

"In my job there's a lot of travel and bursts of high-energy activity when there's a competition, then quiet downtime in between. I used to find the downtime boring, and go looking for trouble, but now I'm learning to enjoy it. Jesse's showing me how. He loves being settled on his own ranch and spending all day with his animals."

"Being a bull rider must be quite a rush."

"Yeah," Bowie turned his head to look at her. "I'm kind of an adrenaline junkie." He grinned. Their faces were close together, looking directly at each other. He looked at her mouth, then leaned slowly toward her.

Their lips touched and Lucy felt a tiny spark of electricity as her lips parted. It was a gentle kiss, soft, hesitant.

They opened their eyes and looked at each other for a second. Bowie's green eyes had darkened, and his face had a strange expression on it, almost a look of surprise.

Before Lucy could cover her confusion with a meaningless comment, Bowie turned his whole body toward her, circled her tightly with his arms and kissed her again.

This time his kiss held no hesitation. It was full, deep, his tongue licking the inside of her lips, his mouth moving over hers hungrily.

Lucy's whole body came alive with sensation. Her breasts tingled and heaviness gathered in her belly. Her arms closed around his neck, fingering the hair at his nape, drawing him toward her. Their tongues met, dancing together as their mouths moved hotly over each other.

Bowie's hand roved over her body, enjoying the full curve of her hips, touching her belly, and rising up to her very tender breasts. Lucy's lips parted in a tiny moan as his fingers ran over her nipple, and he closed his lips over hers, kissing her harder, heating her blood.

Lucy suddenly remembered that they were in a public place. There was no one else outside but people could surely see them from the veranda if they glanced in the right direction. She pulled away, startled at the way she'd lost herself in the kiss.

She tucked her hair behind her ear, a nervous gesture, trying to distract herself from the alarming physical sensations coursing through her body. She felt exposed in her form hugging dress, and longed to be able to draw a shawl over it and cover herself.

Bowie had half smile on his lips. Pure lust glazed his eyes, and his hands rested gently on her hips.

"You are so beautiful." He lifted a hand to her hair and gently played with one of her curls. "I've said that before haven't I? Looking at you is making all my good lines go out of my head. A body like yours could drive a man crazy."

"It's just the dress," Lucy stammered. No one had ever accused her of having a fantastic body before. She didn't want Bowie to get the impression that out of the dress she was some kind of supermodel, then he'd be disappointed for sure.

Was he going to see her out of the dress? He certainly seemed to want to. And Lucy's body was telling her that it wanted to feel this man touching it again, touching it all over, all night long.

"No, it's not the dress. It's you. You are a very lovely woman, and a strong one too. I like that."

Bowie stood up and extended a hand to help her off the swing. Were they going back to his room? Lucy had decided that as far as Bowie wanted to take her, she would go there with him. This was her chance to live a fantasy, to be a queen for a night, to go home with memories that would warm her for a lifetime.

She rose from the chair and he led her across the grass. Her body was heavy and languorous and she felt a little like Mae West as she swayed across the lawn in her tight dress and high heels. The moon had vanished behind a cloud and the darkness of the night was now broken only by the tiny lights in the trees and the glow from lanterns hung around the ranch grounds.

They reached a brick paved path and Bowie led her along it.

"Are you staying in one of the villas?"

"Yes, the one with the blue door, facing the garden." Goodness, he wanted to take her to her room. She wasn't sure what kind of shape she'd left it in. She'd barely unpacked so it probably wasn't too much of a mess. Hopefully she hadn't left her underwear on the floor.

As they walked toward her villa, Lucy's heart thumped in her chest. Would things get hot and heavy? Would he know that she was a virgin?

She certainly wasn't going to tell him, he would feel too much pressure on him. If they did have sex, would she bleed or cry out in pain?

No matter what happened, she was ready. Twenty-seven years of going home alone was quite long enough.

Lucy's hand shook as she drew out her key and opened the door. She turned to Bowie, wondering how you invited a man into your room when you barely knew each other. Maybe she could offer him a coffee? There was a coffeemaker somewhere around.

He leaned in and gave her a gentle kiss. "Sleep

tight my beauty. We've got a long day ahead of us tomorrow."

Then he turned away from her and walked back along the brick path.

Lucy stood in the doorway open mouthed. He was leaving her all alone, fired with desire, and a longing to be touched.

Twenty-seven years and counting. Tonight was not going to be her night after all.

3

In the morning Lucy woke up and wondered if she'd dreamed the whole thing. Perhaps she'd just gone to dinner by herself, drunk a little too much wine and fallen asleep to have a wild fantasy about meeting a sexy, green-eyed adventurer who thought she was beautiful. It certainly was the stuff of dreams.

She got out of bed and wandered into the adobe tiled bathroom. She'd forgotten to wash off the eye shadow and lipstick from last night, and the effect was not too flattering. It was probably a good thing that Bowie hadn't stayed the night after all.

She washed her face and studied it in the mirror. Yikes, those yellow highlights—for yellow was how they appeared under the incandescent light—did not do her complexion any favors. She was definitely going to need to wear makeup again to keep from looking excessively ruddy.

She applied it carefully, smoothing and evening her complexion with foundation and powder, and lining her eyes with shadow and pencil, the way she'd done in high school. She felt sad for her younger self, that hopeful girl who wanted so much to fit in with the popular kids that she'd let them make a victim of her. They'd drawn into their circle, inviting her to parties and connecting with her on social media purely to make fun of her.

It had been weeks before a true friend took her aside to explain what was going on. She'd staunchly denied it, then slowly and painfully realized her friend was right. Her teenage self would have soaked her pillow with tears if she'd known that she'd still be single, and a virgin, all these years later.

She didn't run across single men too often in her life. She'd never dare to risk something like internet dating where you had no idea if the other person was who they said they were. Most of the clients at her barn were female, and aside from Luis, who was married, and Gordon the farrier, who was gay, she rarely had the opportunity to exchange more than a few words with any men.

Her phone rang and she answered it quickly, half expecting to hear that voice again, male, a little husky, with a laugh or a smile winding itself through the words.

"Hello," she said. Her voice cracked, and the second part of the word came out as a squeak. *Very sexy, Lucy*. Luckily, the caller turned out to be Val, her best friend, who had bullied her into taking this trip and threatened her with death, or at least relentless nagging, if she didn't have a good time.

"So, did you meet anyone yet?" Trust Val to get straight to the point.

"Yes, lots of people. The place is quite full." Lucy smiled to herself.

"Lucy," Lucy could hear Val's voice rising in preparation for one of her mother-hen scolds, "I don't want to hear about how you decided to eat dinner in your room because you thought it would be more relaxing. You promised you were going to get out and mingle."

"I mingled."

She felt a little shiver, as she remembered how Bowie had looked at her as she entered the room.

"And?"

"And I ate dinner." *With a man.* She pictured his strong hand crushing her lobster claw beneath his glass, handing it back to her broken into pieces while he looked at her with those heart-melting green eyes.

"And?"

"And I danced the mambo and kissed a man and invited him back to my room."

Val hesitated. "You did eat dinner in your room, didn't you?"

Not surprising that Val didn't believe her. She didn't believe it herself. She frowned at herself in the mirror when she remembered how disappointed she'd been when Bowie left. She'd been ready and willing to do anything he wanted.

Shocking really, she'd never have thought herself capable of wanting to sleep with a man on the first night she met him. She was ready for a little adventure, but she'd been thinking more along the lines of an exciting flirtation, a romantic dance, not dragging a man back to her room and being crushed when he didn't want to stay.

Bowie had done something to her that she didn't understand at all. When he'd touched her on the dance floor, she'd felt a charge flowing through her whole body. She'd felt connected to Bowie through the vibrating music, their fingers touching, their hips brushing against each other as he turned her, his hand on the bare skin of her back.

And then when he'd kissed her.

Lucy blew out a little sigh. That kiss was something else. She felt a little tingle in her fingers and toes just remembering. Bowie had definitely touched a nerve that she hadn't realized was there.

"Lucy?"

"I'm still here. And I really did kiss a man last night." She smiled, imagining Val's mouth forming into that surprised O that made her look like a cartoon fish.

"Who?"

"His name is Bowie. He's a great dancer and an even better kisser."

"Did you sleep with him?"

"You don't beat around the bush, do you? No, I didn't sleep with him."

Not because I didn't want to.

Maybe he'd a long day or wanted to conserve his energy for the trail ride. Or perhaps he'd intended to sleep with her but changed his mind on the way to her room.

"What does he do?"

"He's a bull rider."

"What?! I watch bull riding on TV all the time. What's his name?"

"Bowie West."

"Are you kidding me? That guy's gorgeous! Those green eyes are to die for. And his body..." Val let out a low whistle. "You are kidding me, aren't you?"

"You don't have to believe me. I suppose you think someone like Bowie West wouldn't be interested in me." She couldn't believe it herself. Maybe she had dreamed the whole thing.

"Lucy, you're gorgeous, as I'm always trying to tell

you. Maybe now you'll believe me. I've got to go take Sean to the school bus. Be sure to sleep with him tonight, okay?"

"Okay, anything you say Val."

She wondered if she would sleep with him tonight, or if she'd even get to kiss him again. She'd find out today since they were going on the trail ride together. What would she do if he acted as if nothing had happened between them? She wasn't sure how she'd be able to cope with that.

She recalled that startled look she'd seen in his eyes after their lips first met—he'd felt something spark to life between them.

But he'd turned away from her so casually, wishing her a good night's sleep and walking away without a backward glance. Maybe electrifying kisses were par for the course with him. Maybe he kissed a different girl every night.

For all she knew he headed back to the dance floor to look for someone more glamorous and exciting to spend the night with.

What a predicament she'd gotten herself into. Yesterday was full of promise for a glorious, relaxing vacation. This morning she was already pining like a lovesick calf for some man she'd met only a few hours before.

Get real, Lucy, this is supposed to be fun! If Bowie greeted her casually, dismissively, she would try not to be too disappointed. She wasn't going to let it spoil her vacation.

She'd have a great ride, and a great night out under the stars, regardless of whether Bowie West wanted to kiss her again or not.

Bowie woke up in his room shortly after sunrise. Ouch, he needed a cold shower and bad. All the blood in his body had deserted his brain and limbs and wherever else it might be needed, and concentrated itself between his legs.

Lucy had set his imagination and body on fire— how? Yes, she was pretty, yes, she had a sexy figure, but then so did lots of other women and they didn't torment him in erotic dreams that disturbed his sleep all night long.

Something about her was different. When their lips met in that first hesitant kiss, a cracking explosion—like thunder—had shot through his body. He'd opened his eyes with the shock of it, and there she was looking at him with those big brown eyes that looked like a well he could dive into and happily drown in.

If he'd been his normal self, and she'd been the type of woman he usually hooked up with, he'd have brought her back to his room for a wild night of sex, perhaps with a couple more to follow, then they would have said *adios* and gone their separate ways.

Somehow he couldn't do that to Lucy. He wasn't sure how he knew, but he could tell that she didn't have a lot of experience with men. There was something sweetly naïve and unstudied about the way she tucked her hair behind her ears, or tugged at her dress as if she wasn't used to wearing one.

Lucy's eyes were very dark brown, almost black, and fringed by thick lashes that blinked nervously when she looked at him.

Her lips were unbelievably sensual, and the habit she had of occasionally biting her lower lip, as if unsure of what to say, was unbearably charming and erotic.

And her body was a marvel. Every part of it full and rounded, sensual and womanly, yet muscular and athletic at the same time. It was the type of body that you could lose yourself in—a new continent waiting to be explored.

Lucy, Lucy, Lucy, what have you done to me? He looked down at his problem which was not going away.

He could have stayed with her last night. He could see when she opened the door to her room that she wanted him to. And boy had he been tempted.

But he didn't trust himself with her. He didn't want to hurt her. He didn't want to love her and leave her and that was the only thing he knew how to do. He'd been a burr in his dad's side since he could walk and talk because he just couldn't play by someone else's rules. He'd broken his mom's heart running off to join the rodeo and taking his brother Jesse with him. When a relationship reached the point where the other person wanted to know where he'd be that night, he got the itch to run. He'd probably broken hearts in every state west of the Mississippi.

If Lucy's heart had to be broken, then let someone else break it.

Lucy spent the morning sitting under a wide umbrella watching a natural horsemanship clinic taking place in the ring. Three women had trailered in their problem horses, and Jesse gave them strategies and worked with them as a group. She admired his gentle and encouraging approach with both the horses and the humans, and resolved to try some of his techniques out on her horses when she got home.

She glanced around regularly for any sign of

Bowie, but he didn't appear. The trail ride began at 1 p.m., so she planned to eat the buffet lunch then head over to the stables to meet the other members of the group.

When she packed she'd planned on wearing jeans and a T-shirt for the ride and bringing a sweatshirt in case it got cold at night. Now that she knew Bowie was going to be there she wanted to look a little bit more glamorous.

She fished around in her suitcase until she found the cute shirt she'd brought with her. It was fitted, but not too tight, and had short sleeves and a collar that revealed a hint of cleavage but nothing embarrassing. It looked good with her jeans.

Not bad, a sexy cowgirl look, she thought as she studied herself in the mirror. She'd probably spent more time looking in the mirror on this vacation than she had in the past ten years. But wasn't her regular old self, she was Vacation Lucy, a little bit more glamorous and exciting; the kind of girl who interesting things happened to.

Lucy couldn't help scanning the dining room surreptitiously as she helped herself to soup and a salad. No sign of Bowie or Jesse. Every time someone new entered the room she glanced up, adrenaline surging. Hopefully no one noticed.

After lunch, she walked toward the barn, her heart fluttering with nerves and anticipation.

Would Bowie smile at her, flashing those dangerous green eyes? Would he say "Hey, beautiful," acknowledging their romantic encounter the previous night?

Or would he ignore her, trying to pretend that they

had never met? Might he even fail to recognize her, since she was no longer wearing The Dress?

She hoped for one of the former, but steeled herself for one of the latter.

She introduced herself to the wrangler who would be leading the trail ride—Jack, a young man of twenty or so, handsome and a little shy. She guessed he was probably new to the job.

He showed her to her horse, a big black-and-white paint called Pedro. Lucy tacked up Pedro, who also showed her just where he liked to be scratched.

Jack fastened the bedroll and saddlebags to her saddle, and helped the other two members of the ride who had shown up, a young couple from California called Ben and Dana.

At last, Bowie arrived. Lucy blinked and looked away, busying herself with altering her stirrups, as her pulse rate rose rapidly.

"Hi, Lucy." He tipped his straw cowboy hat in a gentlemanly greeting. He looked devastatingly handsome in a loose-fitting shirt tucked into faded jeans.

"Hi, Bowie," Lucy did her best to sound casual. "I wasn't sure if you were going to make it."

Nice one, Lucy. Now he would know that she'd been thinking about him and worrying whether he would come. So much for appearing cool and nonchalant.

"I went to an auction to look at some bulls. I only just got back."

"That sounds like fun." She wished he'd asked her to come. But then why would he? They barely knew each other. "Did you buy one?"

"Not today. I'd better get tacked up so I don't hold up the ride."

Lucy noted that Bowie saddled his horse quickly and expertly. She found herself sneaking glances at him as she finished buckling her saddlebags and tightening her cinch.

His tanned hands moved nimbly, altering the fastenings on his own saddle, addressing his horse with a casual ease that showed her he was comfortable and experienced with horses.

Great, yet another thing about him that was irresistible.

"Follow me, y'all." They all mounted and Jack guided them out onto the trail. The horses rode in single file at a walk as they headed up a dirt track into the hills.

Jack rode in front, then Dana, then Ben, followed by Lucy. Bowie rode behind her. She was conscious of his eyes upon her as she sat in the saddle, trying to relax and enjoy seeing the countryside.

After about half an hour of walking in shady woods, they did a gentle jog for a while. Lucy couldn't help but notice that Ben and Dana didn't look too experienced. They'd probably be fine as long as the horses stayed in a single file.

As they entered an open field, Jack asked them if they'd like to try a canter. Lucy and Bowie eagerly said yes, though Jack and Dana declined. They looked pretty shaken up by the slow trotting.

Lucy urged her horse forward out of the single file, and once they got past Jack he eagerly struck out over the ground in an energetic lope. Lucy could hear Bowie catching up to her, and she couldn't resist adding speed.

Pedro responded swiftly, picking up the pace until he was covering ground at a gallop. She could hear the hooves of Bowie's horse hitting the ground behind her, gaining on her, and she slowed her horse a little, then let out a little whoop and turned to look at him.

He was grinning, his hat pushed back a little, as they slowed their horses to a trot and rode side by side.

"Ride 'em cowgirl," he called.

Lucy laughed. "This is fun!"

"It sure is. I could have caught up with you, but I was enjoying the view from behind too much."

"Oh, really?" So he was still flirting with her. Lucy felt a little flush of pleasure. Just the way he looked at her made her feel sexy. Their horses pranced around each other, ready to continue running. Bowie and Lucy were both a little breathless.

"Well, cowboy, if you like eating my dust so much I'll let you eat a little more of it. Come on, I'll race you back!"

She struck out, smiling, knowing he would follow her.

"Now that you've challenged me you know I have to beat you," called Bowie's voice from behind her, over the accelerating hoof beats of his horse. As he passed her at a gallop on his larger, more powerful horse, he turned his head in her direction and shouted, "But I'll miss the scenery."

4

They stopped under a grove of trees to eat some biscuits and lemonade. Bowie was solicitous with Lucy, refilling her cup, passing her a napkin. It was an interesting dynamic since the ride consisted of them and the other couple, who were newlyweds. Bowie and Lucy were naturally paired off.

"Did you know Lucy owns her own ranch?" Bowie asked Jack as he brushed biscuit crumbs from his jeans.

"No, she didn't mention that." Jack looked at Lucy, "What are you raising?"

"It's not that kind of ranch. It's a livery stable really."

"Nice." Jack nodded.

"She has twenty-three horses," said Bowie.

Jack whistled. "That's more than Singing Pines has."

"They're not all mine," said Lucy, "Most of them belong to my boarders."

Lucy thought it was funny that Bowie seemed to be proud of her, even though he didn't know her well and had never been to her ranch. Apparently he didn't want Jack to think she was just another dude. It was sweet that he wanted the others to admire her, as if she were his girlfriend or something.

Or something.

They rode the rest of the afternoon on winding trails that took them high into the hills. When the sun hung low in the sky, Jack guided them to a beautiful spot by a lake, where they picketed the horses on a line between two trees and set up camp for the night.

They ate a meal of sausages, beans and cornbread, heated over an open fire. No food had ever tasted better after the exertions of the day.

Bowie passed her a plate of crackling-hot sausages. "Here, have another."

"I'm not sure I should." She'd had two already.

"Up to you, but I appreciate a woman who enjoys her food. There's nothing more annoying than taking a girl out to dinner and watching her pick over a salad with a hungry look in her eyes."

"Especially when that salad is costing you seventeen dollars," chimed in Ben.

Dana looked like she mostly ate salad. She was California beautiful, willowy with straight blonde hair and a golden tan that was probably sprayed on to preserve her dewy complexion. And she was nice, too. She had big, watery blue eyes that almost always rested on Ben, and he seemed to adore her as much as she did him.

The newlyweds made everyone smile. They finished each other's lines and laughed at each other's lame jokes like a couple that had been married for decades rather than days.

Lucy wondered if she would ever have that kind of easy, mutual adoration with a man. Unlikely, and certainly not with someone like Bowie, though he was gamely acting as if they were a couple. She should be embarrassed by it or affronted at his familiarity, but she wasn't. It was nice to be flattered and teased, treated like a lady, even if it was only a charade.

After dinner Jack led them in a round of spooky stories. Bowie told of a time he'd been trail riding in the desert and had camped out in an old cliff dwelling, only to be awoken by a beautiful Anasazi spirit.

"I opened my eyes and looked up into her face, which hovered over me in the moonlight. Her skin was translucent, you could see the skull beneath it, and her eyes were black, empty hollows—"

Bowie paused and looked around the circle for dramatic effect. Then he leaned toward Lucy, who was sitting next to him, and touched her arm. She felt a delicious shudder of fear mingled with desire.

"She leaned over to kiss me with her cold mouth and I wanted to roll away, but I couldn't move." He widened his eyes. "I was turned to stone."

He picked up his beer and took a large swallow. "So I had to let her have her wicked way with me. She didn't seem too satisfied, but I suppose that's a hazard when you turn your lovers to stone. Luckily, one of the other riders tripped over me in the morning and had the kindness to chip me free." His eyes twinkled with mischief.

"And now you're just a rolling stone," teased Ben.

"That gathers no moss," said Bowie with a wink.

And don't you forget it, thought Lucy. It would be all too easy to get used to this. To having him flirt with her and brush against her and maybe even put his arm around her to warm her in the night air. But it wasn't real, and it wasn't going to last. She had no intention of making a fool of herself trying to be the moss on Bowie West's stone.

Lucy made up a tale of a headless horseman arriving at her ranch one night. Though nobody looked too scared, they got a good laugh out of her account of scolding him for galloping around the arena without a helmet.

After the stories, Jack led them in singing some classic cowboy songs. Bowie sang softly, his voice getting lost amid the others, and Lucy was relieved to find something he wasn't talented and confident at.

One song they sang was an old country classic that Lucy remembered learning back in elementary school. As she sang it she realized with some chagrin that it was about a simple and innocent girl being led astray by a handsome rogue. She glanced at Bowie while she sang and as the firelight flashed in his green eyes, she wondered if the girl in the song had wanted to be led astray as badly as she did.

The way Bowie looked at her, she had a feeling that he would be more than willing to lead her astray. His eyes rested on her in unabashed appreciation while she sang, and several times she noticed them flick toward her even when she wasn't the center of attention.

Lucy couldn't help stealing glances at Bowie as he leaned back against a tree, looking up at the sky or into the firelight, listening to the music. When he caught her peeking, she saw a smile creep into his eyes and curl his lips up at the corners before he looked back toward the fire.

What was he doing? Bowie wondered silently. He'd promised himself that he wasn't going to seduce

Lucy. Was he such a cad that he just couldn't help himself? He could tell that she was interested in him. Was he unable to resist taking what she offered?

No, it was something a little different.

He wanted her to feel special. The newlyweds were laughing together and hugging each other, their love for each other obvious to all. He wanted Lucy to have that same reassurance of being wanted, of being cherished. He wasn't sure why it was so important to him to make her feel special. Maybe he just enjoyed seeing her face light up with that pretty smile that made her dark eyes sparkle like polished onyx.

He supposed there was nothing wrong with flirting a little, treating her like the belle of the ball. The important thing was not to act on it. He'd have to make sure that he kept his hands to himself, which was not going to be easy with curves like that inviting his hands to roam over them.

After a while they unpacked their bedrolls and laid them on the ground. Bowie laid his right alongside Lucy's. She was glad that he seemed to still be interested in her. It felt good to have him flirting with her, to see the others smiling at how much he liked her.

"Sweet dreams, Lucy. I know mine will be."

Bowie stretched out on his back, his hands behind his head. As he shifted position a little, his shirt started to come untucked from his jeans. Lucy felt a heat rising below her belly as she thought of slipping her fingers into his jeans right in the warm place that shirttail had just departed from.

She wanted him to make love to her. She wanted to make love to him.

They couldn't do anything tonight, of course. Even Dana and Ben were sleeping fully dressed, curled up close to each other. But tomorrow night was a different story. If she and Bowie didn't make love, then it wouldn't be because she hadn't tried.

Gazing at Bowie's lithe body in the moonlight would keep sleep at bay for a long time. With a silent sigh, she rolled onto her other side.

As she settled comfortably into her new position, she heard Bowie shift closer toward her. Then she felt his hand rest gently on her waist the way it had when they were dancing.

A wave of desire rose through Lucy, warming her from head to toe. It wasn't uncomfortable. In fact, it was strangely relaxing. Somehow having Bowie's warm hand on her body soothed her, it felt just right. With a smile on her lips, Lucy closed her eyes and drifted off to sleep.

The next morning, sleepy-eyed and barefoot, they sat around a cooking fire and had scrambled eggs and biscuits with coffee for breakfast.

"Who's up for a dip in the lake?" asked Jack.

"I didn't bring a swimsuit," said Lucy. "I didn't know we needed one."

"Who needs a swimsuit?" said Dana, eagerly peeling off her jeans and T-shirt and splashing in wearing her sleek mauve underwear. Ben followed her and the lovebirds were soon frolicking in the clear lake water.

Bowie looked at Lucy for a moment and the beginnings of a smile curled one side of his mouth. He didn't say anything. He unbuttoned his shirt quickly and pulled it off, then slipped out of his jeans, revealing a startling array of tanned, toned muscles. Lucy stood watching him in amazement, trying to prevent an embarrassing grin from spreading over her face.

She couldn't help tracking Bowie with wide eyes as he ran headlong into the warm water. He submerged himself completely then rose up, shaking water from his hair like a dog. His laughter was infectious.

"Come on in, Lucy!" He called. She shook her head. She didn't fancy the idea of wet underwear for the rest of the trail ride, and she didn't particularly want him to see her unclothed body in the harsh light of day. She helped Jack pick up the breakfast items and pack the bedrolls back behind the saddles. The horses had been tied up all night and now they snorted and stamped with impatience.

"The horses seem pretty lively this morning."

"Yeah," Jack grimaced, "a night in a new environment can make for an exciting morning. When I take that line down they'll be red hot and ready to go."

"Do you think the newlyweds will be able to handle them?"

"I sure hope so. They said that they were experienced riders when they signed up for the trail ride."

"I shouldn't think either of them has been on a horse for more than an hour in their lives."

"I know. I shoulda known better." Jack shook his head. "Jesse warned me that some people lie about their ability to impress their friends or avoid getting stuck with an 'old nag.' Live and learn, I guess. I'm sorry I've had to keep the group in single file, but I'm afraid to let one of their horses get out ahead and get crazy."

They set off at a walk, but the horses were so jumpy that Jack soon led them into a slow trot to try and burn off some of their steam. Ben had trouble following the motion of the trot and bounced in his saddle, pulling hard on the reins and yelling at his horse to slow down, which made his horse agitated.

As they reached an open plain of grass, Lucy was about to ask Jack if she and Bowie could have a quick canter when Ben's horse decided it had had enough. It broke from the line and took off at a gallop. In a panic, Dana let out a cry and Jack whirled around and grabbed the reins of her horse before it could bolt, too.

"Stay here," called Bowie to Jack, as he took off over the grass toward Ben's fleeing horse. He pushed his horse into a gallop, but Ben's horse had stretched out and was halfway across the open field.

"These horses are dangerous maniacs," said Dana, her voice shaking.

"These horses are great mounts for intermediate riders, which you and Ben said you were," replied Jack quietly.

The two horses had disappeared out of sight in a grove of trees, and Lucy hoped that Ben wouldn't get struck by a low branch or fall off on a rock.

She felt bad for Jack, who would probably take some heat if Ben got injured, even though he'd lied about his experience.

After a few minutes they heard the sound of hooves in the distance. Jack let out a whistle of relief to see Bowie and Ben emerging from the trees, with Bowie leading Ben's horse by the reins.

Ben was shaken but covered it up by saying how

exhilarating the ride was. He told Bowie he could give him the reins back now. Bowie looked at Jack, who shook his head.

Jack dismounted, attached lead ropes to the halters on Ben and Dana's horses, and said that he would be leading them back to the ranch. Lucy offered to lead one of them and Jack gratefully accepted.

The remainder of the ride was quiet. Ben and Dana obviously felt pretty foolish for spoiling the ride for everyone else, but Lucy soothed them by saying that it was getting too hot for the horses to do much more than a walk anyway. It was kind of a relief to discover that the perfect couple wasn't quite so perfect after all.

"You saved the day," said Lucy to Bowie once they'd dismounted back at Singing Pines. They'd ridden in a loop, and the return journey was shorter than the previous day's ride.

"Yeah. I could see it coming the way Ben kept yanking on the horse's mouth. It's amazing that he stayed on and lucky his horse stopped to eat some grass. He's got a good story to impress his pals back in California though, so he's probably not too beat up about it." He pushed his hat back and frowned slightly. "Would you have dinner with me tonight?"

"Yes, I'd love to." Lucy grinned from ear to ear and bent over her saddlebag to hide her elation. She hoped she didn't sound too eager. Maybe tonight would be the night she'd been waiting for—for twenty-seven long years.

5

Lucy took a shower and relaxed in her room. She ordered a sandwich from room service as a late lunch so she wouldn't be too starving at dinner. As she lay on her bed, wearing nothing but her bra and panties, she wondered if she'd be lying there with Bowie that night.

They'd arranged to meet in the dining room at eight, and as that time drew nearer Lucy started to sense moths fluttering around all parts of her body. How would she feel if she ended up back here alone again?

Think positive, Lucy!

She put on some sexy underwear she'd bought for the trip. She decided to wear the black dress again, since nothing she'd brought with her gave her the same confidence. She added a pretty coral necklace and made up her face again.

She looked good; she felt good. Hopefully Bowie would think so too.

As she entered the dining room Bowie rose to greet her from the table he'd chosen near an open French door.

"Hi, Lucy." He pulled back her chair and poured her a glass of champagne. Lucy couldn't help smiling at how his gentlemanly manners contrasted with his rather piratical demeanor.

"How do you feel after the trail ride?" he asked.

"Good. I guess that since I ride every day, doing a bit more riding hasn't stretched my muscles too much. How about you?"

Bowie made a grimace. "Not too bad so far, but I bet I'll be paying for it tomorrow. It was worth it though, to sleep out under the stars next to you."

What a flirt the man was!

They selected food from the buffet. Bowie told Lucy he had a loft in downtown Austin where he stayed when he was in town, but he owned a piece of land he hoped to build on one day. She wondered if she'd ever see them.

Doubtful. Even if he did invite her, it was hard for her to get away from the horses for more than a few hours.

It was a nice fantasy that their relationship had a future, but all she needed was one glorious night. Anything after that would be icing on the cake.

"Yeah, Smokey's been with me since college." She showed him a picture of her big gray gelding on her phone while they ate dessert and drank coffee. "He's nearly twenty-four now, but he's still the most willing horse you could meet. And he has a passion for watermelon. You can't eat it anywhere near him. He'll knock you right over to get to it if he has to."

"I might get into wrestling match with him then," said Bowie, raising one eyebrow just a little, "Since I like watermelon myself."

"Hmm, you vs. a thousand-pound horse, who would win I wonder?"

"Darlin', you don't know me too well yet. Winning is what I do."

"Not every time, surely?"

"No," he smiled and shrugged. "Not every time. But when I lose it's not for want of trying."

Bowie was a nice guy, and easy to talk to. It was kind of a shame that he was famous bull rider, no doubt with girls thronging around him after every ride, as she could see how she could get to like having him as a friend. No sense doing that though, unless she wanted a broken heart to nurse.

After dinner they hit the dance floor again. The band played a series of Latin numbers, and Bowie and Lucy moved across the dance floor together, their hips swinging to the music. The throbbing rhythms of the drums echoed in Lucy's body and her heart beat faster as Bowie pulled her closer.

His arms circled her waist, and her fingers reached inside the collar of his shirt. She ached to shimmy a little closer and rub against him. Her breasts were alive with sensation, her nipples hard inside her lacy bra. As her hips moved toward his, Bowie always stepped slightly back, taunting and teasing her as they sashayed their way around the room.

"Lets go outside," he whispered roughly, in mid song. He grabbed her hand and headed for the veranda. Once they were away from the dining room lights, he tugged her to him and closed his mouth over hers.

Excitement flashed through her as Bowie's tongue sought hers and danced with it. His hands roved up and down her back, hot on her bare skin, grazing down her spine then slipping slightly inside the soft fabric of her dress.

Fingers woven into his hair, she abandoned herself to the kiss. She sensed his hunger for her, even stronger than her longing for him. She could feel his need, hard and hot inside his jeans, as he pressed his body against her.

At last he pulled his mouth away from hers with what seemed like a considerable effort and gazed at her in astonishment. She'd messed up his hair and she smoothed it gently with her fingers.

Lucy plucked up all her courage. "Shall we go back to my room?" Her voice was barely above a whisper.

He hesitated, parted his lips as if about to say something, and a look of distress wrinkled his brow.

Lucy's heart hammered in her chest.

He's going to say no.

She'd just made a royal ass of herself thinking that he found her irresistible. She should have known better than to think he'd actually want to sleep with someone like her.

"Yes. Let's go." His voice was hoarse, his face revealed conflicting emotions, but apparently he wasn't going to turn down her offer. He grabbed her hand and led her down the stairs from the veranda.

Relief mingled with anxiety. She stepped down onto the lawn, where he cupped her face in his hands and kissed her again, very gently, on the lips. His face looked almost pained. He settled his arm around her shoulders and they walked slowly along the brick path back to Lucy's villa while nerves and excitement warred in her belly.

Once inside, she switched on a small lamp so the room was still dim, with just enough light to avoid bumping into the furniture.

Bowie took Lucy in his arms. He kissed her face, her lips, her cheeks, her chin and her neck, his breath hot on her skin. Her body writhed and twisted with the incredible sensation that each of his kisses sent rushing though her.

As his lips lowered to graze her nipple she felt the breath rush out of her lungs. He pushed back the fabric of her dress and her bra, releasing her breast and eagerly sucking and caressing her tight nipple with his mouth.

Still hugging her close, he guided her to the bed where he settled her down gently and climbed over her. His urgent need written all over his face, he tugged her dress down from her shoulders and bared her breasts.

He pressed his face between them, with a low groan, while Lucy felt all her insides soften and melt in the heat of his desire. He eased her dress down over her legs and ankles and stripped off the skeins of lace she'd thought were so alluring without even seeming to notice them.

"Lucy, Lucy," he said, as he surveyed her naked body, which glowed in the soft lamplight. He kissed her thighs, trailing his tongue up the inside of her leg until he reached her sex.

His mouth closed over her, and she let out a little cry at the unfamiliar sensation. His hands caressed her body, her belly, her breasts, her thighs, as he sucked hungrily, making her shudder.

He unbuttoned a couple of buttons near the collar of his shirt and lifted it over his head. He unzipped his pants and pushed them down along with his underwear.

His body was something else. Hard, tanned, taut muscle that could ride a bull or rope a steer or sit a bucking bronco. Heat flashed through her just looking at it. Then he lowered his body over hers again and kissed her long and hard on the lips.

As they kissed she felt him raise his hips and begin to enter her. Her instinct was to tense her muscles, to hold him at bay, but she willed herself to remain open, receptive.

He entered her slowly—so slowly she could barely feel him moving at all. There was no pain. Lucy felt her hips soften and relax as she welcoming him deep inside her.

Suddenly he stopped moving and pulled out, making her gasp with the sense of loss.

"I forgot..." He slid off the bed and fished in the pockets of his pants. His face creased with desperation, he ripped open a tiny packet and sheathed himself with a condom. "Sorry."

Green eyes wide, he moved back over her again, and he lowered his face to hers with a hot kiss. In a flash he was back inside her, warm and hard, moving with her as she arched her hips toward him and pulled him closer with her hands.

Pleasure roved through her, surprising her with unfamiliar sensations that only seemed to build as Bowie moved inside her. As the rhythm intensified, Lucy saw strange colored patterns dancing behind her eyelids and heard herself making tiny moans.

She closed her legs over his back, pulling him even deeper, and Bowie released a string of guttural sounds and climaxed inside her—which gave her a huge thrill. Her whole body felt heavy and tingled with an odd mix of excitement and relief.

She stroked his hair gently and kissed his face, marveling at how happy she was right here, right now, with this man in her bed.

Her wild vacation dream had come true. At twenty-seven years old she'd made love with a handsome cowboy. She'd been initiated into a world that she'd been looking in on from the outside for a long time. She was almost glad it had taken so long to get to this night, because it was all hers.

He hugged her tight and her heart filled with so much joy she almost thought it would burst. She'd wanted Bowie to make love to her, and he'd granted her wish. She would never forget this magical moment.

What had this girl done to him? Bowie couldn't remember a time when he'd ever felt such a desperate urge to be with a woman.

He'd planned to take her out for a nice dinner, maybe a few romantic kisses, then go back to his room alone, as he did on the night they met. He'd promised himself that he wouldn't use her. She was much too nice a girl for that.

But she'd wanted him to make love to her.

He'd steeled himself to turn away from her caresses, to be gentlemanly to the last. But when she'd asked him back to her room and he'd hesitated, the look of sadness—of the pain of rejection—on her face made him want to seize her in his arms and kiss the sorrow away.

Lucy was a special woman, not someone to take advantage of for a quick fling.

And he was ashamed of the way he'd made love to her. He'd made sure she was aroused, at least he'd taken care of that. But he'd been so eager to be inside her that he'd forgotten to put a condom on. Thankfully, he'd remembered before things got out of hand, but what kind of lunatic behavior was that?

He'd planned a long, slow session of gentle

lovemaking, of being sure that her needs were satisfied before his own. But like an oversexed boy he'd lost control and exploded only a few minutes after starting to make love to her.

Her body was a miracle. Even in art he'd never seen such a perfectly proportioned physique of womanly curves. The full roundness of her breasts, the gentle curve of her belly, the slope of her hips, everything about her body made him want to touch her, to hold her, to bury himself inside her.

He'd tried so hard to keep himself in check, to make sure that they didn't get into this situation— then when they did, to make sure that he behaved like a gentleman.

But he'd lost control.

The power this woman had over him was shocking and a little frightening.

Relief overwhelmed him now that they'd made love. He'd endured two nights and a day in a agony of sexual torment. Now he was spent, exhausted, the tension drained from his body

He realized with a start that he still lay collapsed on top of her. He'd totally lost track of reality, and time. Hopefully he hadn't been crushing her for more than a few seconds.

He eased himself off her body and settled himself beside her, his head nestled above her shoulder.

With some effort, he opened his eyes. Lucy's face turned toward him and her dark eyes looked into his. Her mouth curved in a gentle smile.

"Thank you," she said.

Thank you? For what? Bowie was the one who should be grateful that he hadn't had to crawl back to his room and stand under a cold shower for half an hour.

"You have a very expressive face," she said. "What are you thinking about?"

His friends always teased him that his face was a mirror of his emotions. He had no idea how other people could conceal them. That was probably why other people could handle touchy business negotiations, and he was much better off clinging to the back of a bull for a few intense seconds. No one expected you to wear a poker face under those conditions.

He realized that he still hadn't said anything. What could he say? He had nothing to offer her. As had already been observed, he was rolling stone, not the white-picket-fence type. He'd been a proverbial bad boy almost before he could walk, and he didn't do relationships. Anyone he knew could tell you that.

"Just thinking about you."

Play your usual role of flirtatious playboy and try to escape without hurting her. Stay long enough to make her feel cherished, then get the heck out of here and save yourself.

Had he truly been thinking about nothing but her? Was he teasing her? Lucy studied his face. He was probably just flirting with her.

He wore a slightly lopsided grin that gave him a piratical look again. The scar on his eyebrow and the weathering of his skin saved him from being too pretty.

He got up and went into the bathroom to remove the condom. His body was beautiful, toned, lean, not overly muscled. His arms and legs were burned to a nut brown and his torso a little paler; a working man's tan—if you could call what he did work.

And he had a tattoo on his shoulder blade. Lucy couldn't quite make out the image in the dim light of the room. When he came back out of the bathroom, she couldn't resist asking for a better look at it.

"I notice that you have a tattoo on your back. What is it?"

He came to sit on the bed and turned his back to her so she could see it. The image was a tiger, quite large and made up of many tiny dark lines. It looked as if the eyes had been green, but the color was faded. The rest of it was the usual blue-black of a tattoo that has been there a while.

"It's a beautiful drawing. It looks a bit Chinese."

"I had it done in Thailand."

"How old were you?"

"Nineteen." He turned to her and grinned. "I guess it's lucky I didn't get a naked woman tattooed on me or a giant snake that would scare people. I was a crazy kid back then."

"I thought you had to be twenty-one to get a tattoo?"

"Not in Thailand." Mischief sparkled in his eyes.

"What were you doing there?"

"Traveling. After I dropped out of college I took off to see the world. I went around it a few times until I got the crazy notion to grab a bull by the horns. My first bull ride was in Mexico, and like the thrill junkie I am I got hooked right away."

"And made a career out of it. It does seem like the perfect job for you." Lucy smiled. It was impossible to visualize Bowie in an office. Just the thought made her picture a caged tiger.

"Yeah, it's been fun. And I got my more sensible

brother, Jesse, hooked, too. I can't do it forever though." Still lying stretched out on the bed, he looked up at the ceiling. "At some point I'm going to be losing more often than I win and I'm going to have to be man enough to call it quits. Jesse's done a great job transitioning into civilian life so maybe I can too, one day. Not this year, though." He laid a soft kiss on her lips that sent warmth cascading through her. "I have a world championship to win first."

"What we should probably both do next is get some sleep. I'm starting to feel the effects of that trail ride."

"Yeah, me too. I should go back to my room, but maybe I'll rest here for a few minutes before I take off." He moved toward her and put his arm around her. Lucy snuggled closer to him and relaxed, enjoying the warmth of their nestled bodies.

In less than a minute Bowie's breathing became slower, deeper, and soon he was asleep. Lucy smiled to herself at how relaxed and expressionless his face was in repose. He looked gorgeous, his sun-streaked hair ruffled and his sensual lips parted, as if inviting a kiss.

She resisted the urge to kiss him. It was amazing how relaxed she felt with this delicious man wrapped all around her, but she wasn't sure she'd be able to get to sleep after such an exhilarating night.

Hours later she felt someone gently shaking her, a warm breath on her cheek.

"Lucy, I have to go." She cracked her eyes open and could see that Bowie was dressed and standing over her.

"What time is it?"

"It's five. I've got some calls to make. I'll find you

again at a more reasonable hour."

Still drugged with sleep, Lucy nodded. Bowie kissed her gently on the cheek.

"Sleep tight, princess," he murmured, before letting himself quietly out of her room.

Alone again, Lucy lay back on the pillows. She felt a big grin creep across her face. The night had gone just as she'd hoped. She was even glad that he didn't stay until morning. It would have been awkward in the bright light of dawn when he saw her with bedhead and smudged makeup.

So that was sex. She could see what all the fuss was about. It certainly was different. Her body was still warmed and aroused by the experience.

She hadn't bled, and there hadn't been any pain. She probably wasn't technically a virgin because of all the riding she did. Their lovemaking had been short, but it was probably best that way, since it was her first time. It had been short and sweet.

What would happen tomorrow? Would they make love again? She couldn't help hoping that they would.

She knew her relationship with Bowie had no future, but she loved every minute of their brief time together and she wanted it to last as long as possible.

Lucy curled up under the covers. She could still smell Bowie's musky, male scent on the pillows. He was a very sexy man, a green-eyed tiger with a devilish grin.

And just for now, he was all hers.

In the morning Lucy was dancing on air as she walked into the main building on her way to the dining room for breakfast. Her legs ached a bit from the long trail ride, but the rest of her body still tingled with the aftereffects of Bowie's lovemaking.

As she crossed through the lobby, one of the staff approached her.

"Miss Neel, there's a message for you." He led her to the desk, and the receptionist reached under it and brought out a gift basket.

"Who's it from?" asked Lucy.

"Mr. West," replied the receptionist. "He said to make sure you got it first thing."

Lucy smiled. How romantic. She took the basket, which contained a box of Godiva chocolates and a bottle of champagne. Perhaps she would get a chance to feed him those chocolates, one by one, while sipping the champagne tonight.

There was a note in a little white envelope. Lucy balanced the basket on the counter while she opened it.

"Dear Lucy," she read. "I had to leave. Something's come up. I enjoyed our time together. Call me when you get home, Bowie." And his phone number was written along the bottom of the card.

Lucy let out an audible sigh. Her whirlwind romance was over. She wondered if he'd just wanted to get away from her. But if that were the case then he wouldn't have left his number.

Did he really want her to call? Would she call?

Sure, why not?

6

"It was funny." Four days later Lucy chatted with Val while they groomed horses next to each other. "After Bowie left all these other men kept buying me drinks and asking me to dance. It was as if I was suddenly transformed from an ugly duckling into a swan."

"Love will do that to you," said Val with a wink.

"Oh, it was definitely not love. I only spent a couple of days with the guy. He's not the love type." Imagining a real romance with Bowie would be akin to her teenage dream of wanting to hang with the popular crowd. She wasn't fool enough to make that mistake twice.

"He must have been pretty sexy to put that sparkle in your eye. You've looked a little different ever since you came back."

"Maybe that's because now I'm a woman." Lucy bit her lip, looking at Val to see what her reaction would be. Val knew she was a virgin. *Was* being the key word there.

Val stopped pulling her horse's mane and fixed her eyes on Lucy.

"Lucy! You're shocking me. And I'm not easy to shock." The mother of three children by two different husbands, Val insisted that she'd seen and done it all. She narrowed her eyes and placed her hands on her hips. "So you took my advice and slept with him."

"I didn't take anyone's advice. I followed my instincts." For once they'd led her in the right direction. Not into a four-year long-distance relationship with a man who turned out to be gay.

"I admit it, I'm stunned. And impressed. And he's a bull rider! Is he as good-looking in real life as he is on TV?

"I've never seen him on TV but he's pretty sexy." She grinned. "And he has a tattoo of a tiger on his shoulder blade." She got a little shiver of excitement just thinking about him.

"Whoo-hoo! He sounds like something else. Are you going to see him again? Does he live near here?"

"In Austin. When he's in town, at least. But I called him a couple of days ago, and he hasn't called back." That part was a bummer and made her heart sink. Despite her self-imposed warnings, she had gotten her hopes up a little.

"Maybe he's away. Rodeo people travel a lot."

"Maybe."

Another week went by and Lucy still jumped every time her phone rang, but she was beginning to realize that Bowie wasn't going to call.

She'd dyed her hair back to it's usual dark-brown color, since the highlights looked weird and brassy after she'd washed them a few times, especially since she'd put her makeup back into the bottom drawer again.

And she'd settled back into wearing her usual jeans and T-shirts. There was certainly no need for a slinky black evening dress around the High Pastures Ranch.

She'd had her fling, and now life was back to normal. And it was pretty darn good.

Only problem was now she knew what she'd been missing out on: kisses, hugs, heated glances, that tingle of anticipation every time you thought about someone.... She figured she should strike while her iron was still hot and maybe try one of the dating websites. First, she was going to get prepared and get some real contraception—which started with a visit to the ob/gyn. She was overdue for her annual appointment, anyway.

There was an issue of *Cosmopolitan* in the doctor's waiting room, filled, as usual with articles about sex. Lucy had to suppress a smile. It felt good to finally be able to read about sex without wondering if she'd die without having it herself.

She even had the dubious pleasure of ticking of "yes" on the form where it asked if she was sexually active. It gave her a teeny thrill of satisfaction.

Lucy was paying her bill when the doctor asked her to step into her office. Her pulse quickened. Could the doctor be about to tell her she had abnormal cells in her cervix? Surely the results couldn't come back that quickly?

"Ms. Neel, there was something a little unusual in your routine urine test." She frowned and peered at a printout before her. "I know you wrote on the form that you couldn't be pregnant, but it appears that you are about two weeks along."

Lucy's mouth hung open as she tried to process the thought. "But that's not possible, it was only once.... We used a condom."

The doctor shrugged. "Let's do a blood test."

The blood test results removed all doubt. Lucy sat there in stunned silence while the doctor gathered a handful of paper handouts from her desk. "I'm going to prescribe some prenatal vitamins for you. Take one every day. I'm going to give you this packet of information with a few dos and don'ts and what you can expect over the next few weeks and months."

Lucy took the papers. *What?* She was speechless. *Pregnant?* It didn't seem possible.

She had sex one time in twenty-seven years and got pregnant. What kind of luck was that?

Being pregnant was one thing, but at the end of nine months that would translate into something else. A real live baby.

Lucy worried that she was going to be a hazard to other drivers as she drove to the pharmacy to pick up her prescription. While she was waiting for the pharmacist to fill it, she picked up the Austin paper and started to flip though it, trying to get her mind off her predicament.

An item on page five stopped her. As she read it she was stilled by a sense of shock even more numbing than the awful surprise in the doctor's office.

"Bull Rider Still Behind Bars. As we previously reported, the West heir is the prime suspect in a late-night shooting. The victim was found dead in the parking lot of a strip club outside tiny Aileen, Texas, and the bullet has been matched to a weapon found at the rodeo star's residence in downtown Austin."

What? Lucy didn't know Bowie well, but it was hard to imagine him shooting someone. Then again, he did call himself a bad boy, and maybe he wasn't kidding. Perhaps she'd taken a big risk—and made a big mistake—in sleeping with a handsome stranger.

The words jumped around in front of her eyes and she had a hard time reading on.

"Considered a serious flight risk due to his wealth and connections, Bowie West was remanded by the county sheriff's department pending his bail hearing, and recently learned that his request for bail was denied. His legal team is appealing."

Poor Bowie. That explained why he hadn't called. Renewing her acquaintance would hardly be at the top of his list of things to do when he was facing a life sentence.

"Neel, Neel, your prescription is ready," boomed the disembodied voice over the PA system. Folding the newspaper, she made her way to the pharmacy counter in a stunned daze.

Back at home, Lucy had a pounding headache. She'd glanced over all the papers the doctor had given her and read enough to realize that she couldn't take what she had in the medicine cabinet. She was going to have to go out and get some Tylenol, but she didn't have the energy to face the world right now.

She hadn't told anyone about her pregnancy. She didn't even dare tell Val. She didn't want to hear her astonishment, and possibly scolding, or see her shocked expression. She had enough shock coursing through her system already. It was hard to imagine how she could run the ranch while pregnant, let alone with a baby in tow.

And she was going to have to tell Bowie.

He needed another problem right now like he needed a hole in the head.

What a disaster. And it got worse. Bowie wasn't just your run-of-the-mill gorgeous rodeo cowboy. From reading on she'd found that he was the son of a wealthy oil and ranching tycoon and had inherited a big ranch he didn't even live on. He'd probably think she was after his money when she told him about the pregnancy. He'd say it wasn't possible, that he'd used a condom.

Maybe he'd say that it must have been some other affair she'd had during her week at Singing Pines. And she'd have to tell him that he was the only man she'd had sex with in her entire life. The whole thing was going to be very humiliating.

Lucy decided that she might as well get it over with. Head still pounding, she dialed the number that Bowie had scrawled on the note he left her.

The phone rang four times then went to voicemail. Lucy knew she couldn't casually mention that she was carrying his baby in a recording. She wasn't quite sure what she was going to say when she heard the beep.

"Hello, Bowie, this is Lucy, Lucy Neel, we met at the Singing Pines Ranch." Maybe he knew loads of Lucys. "Listen, I read about your legal problems in the paper and I'm sorry to hear about it. I'd like to talk to you, no pressure, just as friends, you know. Please give me a call when you get a chance."

She said her number slowly, then hung up. She didn't think she'd said anything too stupid. Hopefully, he would call. If not, she'd have to keep calling until she got hold of him.

While she wasn't having any classic pregnancy symptoms such as morning sickness, Lucy was tired. After her evening rounds in the barn, she sat down on the sofa to watch the news and fell asleep almost instantly.

Her ringing phone woke her, and she groped her way to it in a groggy state.

"Hello."

"Hi, Lucy, it's Bowie." His low voice jolted her awake.

"Oh, my gosh, Bowie, hi." She struggled to gather her thoughts. "Thanks for calling back. I read about your arrest in the paper. That really stinks."

"That's one way of putting it. I'm innocent."

"I believe you." She meant it, too. Right now the warm and reassuring sound of his deep voice could convince her of anything.

"This is why I left your room early that morning. My attorney called to tell me there was a warrant out for my arrest."

"Are you okay?" she asked. He didn't sound quite like the cavalier, flirtatious Romeo she'd met at Singing Pines. His voice had a distinct edge to it.

"As okay as I can be after spending time behind bars. I'm beginning to know how the bulls feel."

She wanted to laugh but no sound came out. Lucy didn't have the heart to tell him about her pregnancy right now. She'd have to wait for a better time.

"My lawyer finally managed to get me bailed out, and now we have to figure out who actually did the shooting before we go to trial. I'm on the road right now. Too many reporters outside my place downtown and I don't want to deal with them. I'll call you when I figure out where I'm going."

An idea flashed into her mind. A crazy idea. A scary idea. But at least she'd get to tell him face-to-face. "Bowie, would you like to come and stay at my ranch for a few days." This was probably madness. "No pressure, you know, just friends. You can stay away from the city for a while and keep a low profile."

"I'm not allowed outside a fifty-mile radius of the city. How far away are you?"

"I'm only about thirty miles away. Near Denton."

"I know that area." He sighed. "Are you sure I won't be too much trouble?"

"No trouble at all. Do come, just for a few days of rest."

And to learn that you're going to be a father.

"Okay, I'd like that."

Lucy gave him her address and he said he'd arrive around seven o'clock that evening. She'd have plenty of time to do her afternoon rounds, take a shower, and get spruced up before he arrived.

Once she got over an initial bout of recrimination, Lucy was glad she'd invited Bowie to come visit. She had to tell him about the baby. *The baby.* Every time she thought about it, she was shocked all over again.

She touched her tummy in disbelief. Suddenly her life had completely changed and she would be bringing a new person into the world. She'd no idea how she was going to manage, but luckily she still several months to figure it out.

Would she go weak in the knees at the sight of Bowie? She was going to have to keep a cool head and focus on keeping her emotions to herself when she told him about the baby.

Lucy had to feed all the horses, check their water, and make sure everyone was where they should be for the night. She'd finished the feeding, and was scrubbing out a water trough in preparation for refilling it, when she heard a car in the driveway.

She checked her phone. It was 6 p.m. Who would be coming to ride this late?

A vehicle pulled into the turnaround by the house, and, peering through the gap between the barn and the house, Lucy saw Bowie West—one whole hour early—climbing out of a shiny black truck.

For a second she wondered if she could run into the house and hide. She was hot and dirty and had grit under her nails. Of course he looked perfect: tall, tanned and breathtaking in faded jeans and a blue ombré plaid shirt.

Her heart thudded. How was she going to do this?

She lost sight of him behind some bushes as he walked up to the front door to ring the bell.

"Bowie," she called. "I'm over here by the barn." She turned off the hose and left the water trough on its side. There was nothing else for it—now he was going to have to see the real Lucy.

Bowie appeared around the side of the house. She walked toward him and for a second he didn't seem to recognize her. Was the transformation from swan back into ugly duckling so total?

And he had no idea she was carrying his baby.

7

Bowie looked around him while Lucy refilled the fifty-gallon trough. He wasn't sure how he'd thought her ranch would look, but this wasn't what he'd expected. The fences looked fairly solid but were long overdue for painting, and the barn looked like it needed a new roof about two years ago.

Of course the overcast gray sky and his miserable gray mood weren't exactly the right filters to look through if he wanted to see the ranch in a positive light.

The horses were pretty. They were a colorful group, lots of paints and appaloosas.

Lucy looked different than he'd expected, too. Something had changed about her hair, it was darker, maybe. She looked cute though, in her frayed jeans and T-shirt, with her untamed curls blowing in the breeze.

Already he started to feel the burden of his troubles lifting. Coming to visit Lucy was just what the doctor ordered.

He greeted her with a chaste kiss on her cheek. She might be freaked out by the legal mess that had blown up, and he didn't want to intimidate her.

It was hard to keep his hands off her gorgeous

body as his lips touched her warm cheek, but Lucy was the kind of girl where you'd better come on slow and easy rather than hot and heavy. He certainly hoped to have his hands on her later that night.

Lucy had prepared the spare bedroom for Bowie, since she'd promised on the phone that they would be "just friends." She stood aside as he entered and tried not to notice the rush of hormones that happened inside her when he brushed past her. He placed his small bag on the chair, then turned and looked at her expectantly.

"What can I do to help with dinner?"

"What do you think about having a barbeque? We could grill salmon."

"Sounds good." The sparkle in his eyes did something strange to her stomach.

"Why don't you help yourself to a beer or something from the fridge. I need to go get cleaned up." She looked down at her barn clothes with a rueful expression.

"You look fine to me. Don't get dressed up on my account. I don't want to interrupt your routine."

"I'll just have a quick shower. I'll be down in a minute."

Under the warm stream of water from the shower, Lucy closed her eyes. This was going to be even harder than she thought. Why did Bowie have to be so damned gorgeous?

The sight of him climbing out of his truck had made her reel like a giddy schoolgirl. She couldn't imagine how she was going to look into those green eyes and tell him that she was going to have his baby.

She toweled herself dry and looked in her closet.

She'd hoped to have half an hour to figure out what to wear. Bowie had told her not to alter her routine, but she didn't think he would want her to take it so literally as to put on her usual PJ bottoms and college T-shirt.

Of course, that was probably what she should do. She should brush aside all thoughts of her and Bowie as a romantic item and work on building a friendship. They were going to have to be friends if Bowie was to be a part of the baby's life.

There was no question of her and Bowie getting married, she could see that. A web search had proved that he was one of the hottest stars on the rodeo scene, with girls screaming his name after every ride. She couldn't compete with that even if she wanted to—and she didn't want to. She'd grown up sharing her pastor father with everyone in their small town, and it wasn't until she was twelve and her mom was hospitalized for depression that she learned he'd been sleeping with half of them too. The last thing she needed was a man who'd be tempted to stray.

She had to be practical and approach their relationship from a new, more realistic angle.

She put on some black jeans and a pearl gray V-neck T-shirt that stopped short of revealing any cleavage. It was casual, and flattering, but not exactly a come-hither ensemble. It would have to do.

No makeup though. There was no point in dressing up as someone else now. *What you see is what you get, Bowie West.* She knew he could never love her, but she hoped he would like her enough to agree to be a part of the baby's future.

Bowie was sitting on the sofa drinking a beer when

she came downstairs. He jumped up to help her carry the food outside onto the patio, where the wooden table and chairs faced out toward the paddocks.

The setting sun threw pinkish light over the fields and drew the fence shadows out long. They sat and watched the horses moving and munching in the fields.

Lucy turned on the gas grill and sliced some peppers, onions and zucchini to grill with the salmon.

As he settled back into his chair, Bowie let out a long sigh.

"Damn, what a time I've had since I last saw you."

"I saw the newspaper story. I couldn't believe it. I didn't believe it." She wanted to reassure him. "How did it happen?"

"It started while I was with you. I got a call that the sheriff's office in Aileen wanted to talk to me in connection with a shooting. I had no idea what the heck was going on. That's when I told you I had to leave."

"When did they say the shooting happened?"

"That night. Around three in the morning, they say."

Her gut seized. "So you were with me. You did tell them that, right? Why didn't they contact me?"

"I didn't want to spread your private business all around. That had nothing to do with it."

"But they put you in jail! At least that's what the story said."

"My lawyer was finally able to post bail. I don't want your name dragged into it."

Lucy blinked. She wasn't sure if his behavior was heroic or foolish. The grill was hot so she put the salmon and vegetables on it, her brain spinning.

"Who was shot? And why do they think you did it?"

"Her name was Terri Balboa. Apparently, she's some kind of…lady of the night." He frowned. "I've never seen or heard of her before. She was shot at point-black range and died instantly. They found a handgun registered to me tossed into some bushes nearby, and ballistics showed that it was the murder weapon."

"And is it really your gun?"

"Apparently so. I collected them for a while. I used to shoot competitively before my rodeo career took off. They're kept locked in a gun closet in my loft, which I hadn't even opened in months."

"So you think someone broke in and stole it to frame you?"

He shook his head and a frown creased his tanned brow. "I don't know what to believe. If I'd had a break-in that would help, but I haven't—not that I know of. And my fingerprints were on the gun. She'd also called my phone a bunch of times. The police found her number in there, but I swear I never spoke to her."

Lucy remembered his phone ringing during their first dinner together. "Could she be that woman who called you about a prize?"

Bowie frowned. "I'd forgotten about that. And I never had a prize."

"Someone could have made up a fake prize and given her your number just to have her call you and get her number in your phone."

"Damn. It sure looks like someone is trying to stitch me up. I'll mention it to my lawyer."

Lucy blew out. "Do you have a good lawyer?"

"The best. But even calling a criminal defense

lawyer felt like an admission of guilt." He took a deep draught of beer. "At least my family's behind me. My brothers are all calling in every favor they're owed to draw attention to the case and find the real killer. Even my dad, who I've been on the outs with for years, sent me a message of support."

"Perhaps the killer is someone with a personal vendetta against you, someone whose only goal is to hurt you. Can you think of anyone who would hate you that much?"

Bowie looked at her, shook his head, then looked down at the ground.

"I'm sure I've ticked a few people off by beating them in rodeos, I can't think of anyone who would hate me enough to want me in jail."

"Maybe someone who wants you out of the running for the finals that are coming up?"

"Who could be so desperate to win that they'd kill an innocent woman?"

"Maybe she's where you should start? Why did they pick her?"

"Could be the same reasons serial killers choose their victims. From what we've learned so far, Terri Balboa lived alone, earned a meager living as an exotic dancer in a dingy roadside joint, isn't from the area and has no known relatives. She could have just been an easy target."

"Poor woman. Still, maybe there's a connection you haven't figured out yet. I wouldn't leave any stone unturned."

The salmon steaks were done, and Lucy served them with the grilled vegetables and a tangy dill sauce. A question was gnawing at her. "Have you been in trouble with the law before?"

"No. Not like this. I did some stupid stuff when I was a kid but nothing that I would have gone to prison for. I was thrown out of the boarding school that four generations of West men have attended because I just couldn't seem to follow all of their arcane rules."

"Somehow that doesn't surprise me."

"I get bored easily. The nice thing about bull riding is that you only have to do it for eight seconds."

She laughed. "And they're pretty action-packed seconds."

"Even I can't get bored." His mouth tilted into a sexy grin that made Lucy's hear flutter.

Then she remembered her secret. How would Bowie feel about being a father? Someone who got bored easily was not an ideal candidate for the routine day-to-day work of parenting. Most likely she'd be doing that by herself, but she did hope that Bowie would find a place in his life for their child.

Should she tell him now? They were talking quite seriously and it was the kind of news that would feel like a body blow whenever she delivered it.

Her heart started racing and she tried to form the right words in her mind.

You're going to be a father.

I'm having a baby.

Hey, guess what?

Her courage failed her.

Bowie had no idea what was going on in her brain. He looked very relaxed, enjoying his dinner. "I like your ranch."

"Thanks. I love it here. It's a dream come true."

"I can tell. There's an air of contentment about it. Your horses seem happy." He looked out toward the dark shapes moving in the fields. "And your house has a nice cozy feel to it."

"Thanks. I have a lot of projects left to do, but I keep telling myself I have the rest of my life to get them done."

"I think everything's a work in progress. I know I am." As he winked she could see a hint of that piratical mischief that had enchanted her back at Singing Pines.

Tonight she would let him unwind and try to forget about his troubles for a few hours. But tomorrow she would have no choice but to pile yet another trouble on his plate.

Tomorrow she would have to tell him about the baby, their baby.

8

"I usually make one last round to check on the horses before turning in. Would you like to come?"

Lucy and Bowie had carried the plates inside and were planning to find a good movie on TV.

"Sure."

They walked out toward the paddocks, and Lucy silently accounted for each of the horses as they grazed in the dark. She led Bowie into the barn to check on two horses that were stalled.

One was inside because he had a leg injury that he needed to stay off. The second, Dancer, was a new, young horse that was only in the barn to keep the injured horse company.

As they approached the second stall, Lucy had an odd premonition that something wasn't quite right. The movements of the horse sounded agitated.

When she looked into the stall her fears were confirmed. The chestnut mare was biting and kicking at her stomach, writhing in discomfort. As Lucy watched, she buckled her knees and lay down.

Panic spiked through her. She'd lost a horse to colic two years ago and knew the symptoms far too well.

"I think Dancer is colicking. I need to give her a

banamine injection and call the vet. Could you lead her into the arena while I run and get my phone?"

"Of course." He didn't hesitate, or sound even slightly apprehensive. As a rodeo guy he was used to horses as well as bulls. She took a moment to thank her lucky stars he was here to help her.

She haltered Dancer and led her out of the stall, where she kept trying to lie down and roll, a symptom of the agony roiling inside her gut. Colic meant that the intestine had become blocked. It could kill a horse, and fast. The vet had told her to keep a colicking horse walking, because their instinct to roll could actually worsen any twisting in their gut.

Lucy left Dancer walking Bowie, switched on the arena lights, then ran inside to get her phone and the banamine she stored on the top shelf in her pantry. On the way back out, she called the vet and left a message with the answering service.

Bowie was calmly leading Dancer around the well-lit arena, talking to her softly and rubbing her neck and withers. Lucy's heart squeezed at his compassion for the unhappy mare. Bowie held her still while Lucy injected the drug in her neck, then she took the lead rope from Bowie and continued to lead Dancer back and forth. Her own stomach was churning, probably with nerves. When the phone rang ten minutes later, she answered, wordlessly handing the lead rope back to Bowie.

"Dancer's colicking. She was okay when I checked on her at five, but now she's kicking at her stomach and wanting to roll. I gave her banamine, but she still looks pretty bad."

The vet explained that she was in the middle of a difficult delivery that had gone on far too long. The foal was breech and there was a possibility of losing the mare and the foal. She said to keep in touch and she'd be there as soon as she could."

"Damn. She's tied up with a delivery. Usually if the bananmine was going to work it would have by now. Poor baby," said Lucy, stroking Dancer's neck and face. "We're going to make you feel better."

"You don't look so hot yourself. Are you okay?" Concern hung in Bowie's low voice.

"I'm okay." She realized she was holding her stomach, which now felt decidedly queasy. Could this be morning sickness even though it was night? In the panic over Dancer she's forgotten all about the baby. Truth be told she felt a little dizzy, and walking the mare around in circles wasn't helping.

"Lucy, I think you should go inside and lie down. I can look after Dancer. I've walked a horse though many a colic. Besides, she's looking a little calmer."

"Are you sure?" She hated to ask a favor of anyone. It was one of her biggest weaknesses.

"I'm sure. I'll call you if anything changes."

"Okay." She didn't even have the strength to argue. If she didn't lie down she might actually fall down. The arena was starting to spin. "I'll be in the living room and I'll open up the windows so I can hear you."

Lucy hurried inside, clutching her stomach. She could hardly believe that she was leaving Dancer when she was so gravely ill, but she felt pretty bad herself, and sudden mild cramping in her gut scared her.

She lay down on the sofa and curled up in the fetal position, every now and then craning her neck to look out the window to where Bowie talked gently to

Dancer while he walked her. Over the next fifteen minutes or so the cramping eased, and the shaking gradually lessened, but the nausea remained. Was this a normal part of pregnancy, or had something gone wrong?

She'd only just learned that she was pregnant, but already she was strangely attached to the little life growing inside her. She didn't want to lose it.

"Are you trying to attract my attention?" she murmured, stroking her belly. "Are you mad that I'm keeping you a secret?"

It was hard to believe that there was a real person growing in there. She wondered if the baby would have Bowie's green eyes or her dark ones. Would the baby be a girl who loved horses or a boy who wanted to ride bulls? Only time would give the answers.

Or at least she hoped it would. Thank goodness the cramping had stopped. It was probably just her stomach kinking up from the stress and tension of worry about Dancer.

Lucy propped herself up on the sofa and peered out the window. She couldn't make out what Bowie was saying to the mare but it touched her that he was trying to communicate with the suffering animal. Dancer's flashy white socks and pretty blaze glowed in the arena lights, making it easy to see that she did look a lot more relaxed. If she stayed that way when the banamine wore off, then they could relax. Until then...

Lucy awoke with a start at the sound of tires in the driveway. She sat up with a gasp. How could she have fallen asleep when one of her horses was desperately sick?

The pregnancy was really sapping her strength. She

looked out the window and saw Bowie signaling to the vet to come over. Lucy hurried outside.

"I think she's fine now," said Bowie to the vet. He pointed to a fresh manure pile. "I've never been so glad to see a load of crap in my life." He grinned. "Hey, Lucy, Dancer's a lot better. How are you doing?"

"I'm okay, too. I can't believe I fell asleep. Sorry to leave you out here all night long."

"No problem. Dancer and I have been talking about a lot of things, haven't we, girl?"

The vet checked Dancer over and pronounced her fine. Lucy was feeling pretty good herself, so she made breakfast for the three of them as the sun rose up over the fields.

After the vet left, Bowie insisted on helping her with the morning chores, pointing out that she might be coming down with something and assuring her that walking the horse had given him time to reflect and he had more energy than he'd had in days.

"Would you like to ride one of the horses?"

"I'd love to." Bowie smiled. "Which one are you going to pick for me?"

"Hmm, why don't you choose? The ones in these two paddocks are all my babies."

Bowie scanned the field. Her horses were divided into two bands, one of mares and one of geldings, except for a few roughnecks separated into individual pens.

"How about that big black mare over there? She's a pretty mover."

Lucy chuckled. "That's Wonder; she's only three. She's still pretty green and quite a handful. But you're welcome to ride her if you want to."

"I want to."

They brought the mare into the arena, and Lucy went to the tack room to get a saddle and bridle. She left Bowie standing inside the arena gate holding Wonder's lead rope.

When she came back, Bowie and Wonder were no longer by the gate. She instantly worried that Wonder had bolted, but when she looked up she saw them at the other end of the arena.

Bowie had mounted Wonder and was riding her bareback, with just the halter in his hand. His lithe and powerful body moved in sync with the horse's rhythm, almost as if he were a satyr with a horse's body.

Bowie chuckled when he saw Lucy's expression. He trotted Wonder over to Lucy, looking like he had her perfectly under control. "Surely you're not surprised that I can ride bareback."

A smile snuck over her face. His confidence was irresistible. "Go on, show off a little." Wonder started prancing about excitedly, and Bowie looked like he was ready for action too.

They spun and took off across the arena in a flashy trot. Wonder's movements were fluid and confident, as Bowie rode her with no visible effort. His powerful legs urged her forward when necessary, and guided her into turns, and he managed to control her head with gentle movements of his hand on the lead rope.

Suddenly, Bowie urged Wonder forward, heading straight for a barrel that was lying on its side in the middle of the arena.

Lucy raised a hand to her mouth, unsure of what he was going to do. The horse had only had western training and had never jumped. Bowie urged her onward and as they reached the barrel he reached his hands along her neck and Wonder leapt over the barrel effortlessly.

Without looking, at Lucy Bowie slowed the horse to a walk and circled the ring one time, patting Wonder's neck and talking to her softly.

Bowie walked Wonder over to Lucy again. He dismounted in a swift movement and showered Wonder with kisses and pats.

Lucy felt a little flare of jealousy to see her horse receiving Bowie's affection when she hadn't had so much as a touch from him since he arrived.

"She's lovely," he said.

"She certainly likes you. I've never seen her move out so well. That horse has never jumped before."

"Guess she knew how anyway." He shrugged and smiled. "You did say to show off, didn't you? I didn't want to disappoint you."

Bowie's roguish expression and the twinkle in those green eyes made Lucy's stomach leap. Wonder nuzzled him gently, and he returned the horse's caress with his powerful, bronzed hands.

Again Lucy felt a surge of envy, or perhaps it was lust. Bowie moved with such sinuous strength and athletic grace, his body was honed to perfection, and he knew how to use it. That kind of thing could cast a spell on anyone.

Try as she might, Lucy was having a hard time looking at Bowie as just a friend. Her mind might know that was the only sensible course to pursue, but her body had other ideas.

Bowie was wrapped up in looking at Wonder, touching her all over, palpating each part of her body as if he were doing a vet check. Lucy wished she could change places with the horse and be the recipient of those firm, yet gentle caresses.

Stop, Lucy! Keep a cool head. But keeping her feelings under control was easier thought than done. Her whole body tingled with desire for this charming and capable man who had clearly bewitched one of her wilder horses.

They turned Wonder back out with the other horses, then leaned on the fence and watched the herd grazing and playing together under the warm morning sun. The higher fields glowed green with the tips of new spring grass breaking through the ground. The air smelled sweet with the nectar of spring flowers mingled with the musky smell of the horses. The trees had leafed out and the landscape was starting to look lush and glorious after the long, cold winter.

"I own some land near here. Spending time here is making me realize it's about time I did something with it."

"You do?" Who just "owned land" and didn't do anything with it?

"My mom willed it to me when she died. I visited it once years ago with my brothers. It was right near Denton. That's why I said I knew the area. I'll have to find it again."

Lucy blinked. He'd have to *find* his land? If he knew how hard she'd scraped and saved for these few acres he'd probably think she was mad.

"It's not that big. Less than five thousand acres. It's been leased out for cattle to the same farmer since long before I owned it."

"Five thousand acres? I have five acres here, with no zeroes at all, and I thought that was pretty impressive. I guess it's all about perspective." She wanted to sigh. More proof that they weren't even close to playing on the same field.

"You're ranch is perfect, Lucy."

"Oh, it's not perfect. Everything needs painting and the barn needs a new roof. And those are just the obvious problems."

"It's not so hard to buy a little paint and a few shingles."

"The labor to do the work is considerably more than the materials themselves. I'm too busy taking care of the horses to have hours left over for painting."

"You're not telling me you run this place all by yourself?"

"I do."

"With no help at all?" Bowie's green eyes grew wide with disbelief.

"Sometimes I hire Luis, who works on a nearby farm, to help out. He took care of the place when I was at Singing Pines. But most of the time it's just me." He wasn't the only one who thought she was crazy. Her friend Val had begged her to at least hire some high school kids to help out.

"Why don't you hire some help?"

Lucy smiled. "It costs money to hire people, Bowie. I'd rather spend what little money I have on the horses. Besides, I like doing the work myself. I enjoy spending time with the horses and getting to know them all closely. If someone else was taking care of their daily needs it wouldn't be the same."

"You're amazing." Bowie looked at her.

She basked for a second in the glow of his appreciation. "I'm just doing what I love to do."

She gasped when Bowie cupped her face in his hands and he leaned in to kiss her. Their lips met and something exploded inside her. Heat and light and who knows what rushed through her veins and she felt her hands reach around Bowie's back, pulling him to her.

Her body had hungered for this closeness ever since Bowie arrived at her ranch, ever since the first moment she had laid eyes on him.

The kiss was long and soulful and filled her with wonder. Bowie held her tightly, his hands roving up and down her back, playing in her hair. When at last they pulled away from each other, his face wore a rather stunned expression.

"Lucy." He ran his finger gently down the side of her face. "Lucy, Lucy."

She'd no idea what he was thinking. He leaned toward her and kissed her again, this time gently, hesitantly, touching her mouth with his lips, then drawing back, kissing again, then pulling back.

His eyes were open, and Lucy looked into their jade green depths as his mouth danced with hers, touching, enticing, his tongue licking her lips in provocation. When his mouth closed over hers, Lucy felt her body grow warm and soft, sinking into his arms.

Bowie groaned, caressing her, as Lucy allowed herself to melt into him as his kiss and his touch warmed her whole body and shattered her resistance.

As their lips parted and she opened her eyes, she saw Bowie smiling. The stunned expression was gone from his face, replaced by an expression of happiness.

For a brief moment Lucy felt that happiness reflected in her. Their kiss had reignited the passion that flared at Singing Pines. There was something between them that couldn't be denied—a chemical connection, an alchemic brew that filled the air and made her drunk with longing for this handsome man who was no longer a stranger.

Then she remembered.

He wasn't just a handsome man anymore. He was a father-to-be.

And he didn't know it yet.

Telling him about the baby would ruin this magical moment, but she had to tell him. And she had to tell him now, before things got any further out of hand.

Heart pounding, she gathered every ounce of courage she owned. "Bowie, there's something I need to talk to you about.

9

Bowie lifted a brow, humor and intrigue sparkling in his eyes. "What is it?"

"There's no easy way to put this. I'm...well...when we...at Singing Pines—" Lucy couldn't seem to bring herself to say the words.

Bowie's frowned, his carefree expression fading, replaced by a growing look of concern.

How would he react when she told him? Would he be angry? Would he deny it? Would he blame her for dragging him to bed? Would he take her in his arms and say he was ecstatic—that this was what he'd always dreamed of?

Only the last was impossible.

"I'm pregnant."

Bowie looked at her, then he looked away and let out a sharp exhale.

"How far along?"

At least he hadn't called her a liar. But his question showed that he doubted it was his.

"Three weeks. Three and a bit."

It sounded so slight. *Three and a bit.* But there was no such as a little bit pregnant. One day, two weeks, nine months, at the end there was the same result, a living, breathing human being.

"I didn't think they could tell that early." He fixed his green eyes on her, his mind obviously working through the possibilities.

He didn't believe her. Maybe he thought she was trying to trap him. He was rich and she wouldn't be surprised if this had happened to him before.

"I would never have known. I had a routine doctor's appointment and they noticed it in a urine test. Then they did a blood test showed elevated HCG levels. It's a hormone. The levels rise every day from the moment you conceive."

"But I don't understand how I could have—" Bowie shook his head, stared at the ground, then back up at her. "I used a condom."

He *was* going to deny it. To say that she must have slept with someone else.

Her heart seized up and she felt tears rise in her throat with the shame of it. She'd never been with a man in her life before him and now she was exposed to a charge of promiscuity.

"You did, but you didn't put it on until we'd already...you know. It must have been too late by then."

Bowie's expression was unreadable. She knew he was certainly regretting those few minutes of pleasure that he'd kindly bestowed on her.

"I'm sorry, Lucy. I got carried away in the moment."

His green eyes looked right into hers. She saw no hostility there, only confusion. He wasn't denying it. He was taking the blame. Behaving like a gentleman.

Somehow his gracious apology made her guilt worse. She'd wanted him in her bed. She'd craved a night of pleasure, and she'd roped him into her scheme without any thought for what could go wrong.

"It was my fault. I should have protected myself." She did blame herself for that. She felt like an idiot. Such naiveté might be understandable in a breathless teenager, but not a sturdy spinster of twenty-seven.

Bowie scratched his head, looked at Lucy's belly—which wasn't any rounder than usual—then down at the ground. The awkward silence stretched on for what seemed like forever.

"I'm going to keep the baby, Bowie."

Bowie looked at her wordlessly, then nodded.

At least he wasn't going to question her choice to have the baby. But he certainly wasn't jumping forward to offer to be a loving father to it. Had she expected him to? She didn't know what she'd expected. Her hands grew cold.

Lucy crossed her arms over her chest. "I'm a grown-up and I should have been more careful. I wasn't and now I'm going to face up to my responsibilities. I won't come after you for money, Bowie."

Might as well get that off her chest. Sure, money was going to be tight but she didn't want him thinking she'd planned the pregnancy to get a piece of his wealth. He probably wouldn't believe that she had known nothing about it.

"Don't think about the money. I'll take care of you and the baby." His shoulders heaved as he drew in a deep breath.

A bucket clattered over and a horse whinnied. Lucy turned to see what was going on.

"Smokey's knocked his water over. I'll go refill it." She walked away, glad of an excuse to break the tension.

She'd told him. She was glad she'd finally come out and said it. It was a relief to get it off her chest.

Bowie's kiss had taken her by surprise. The unexpected pleasure of it, of melting into his arms, had reawakened her desire for him.

For a brief instant she'd felt warm, safe, cherished.

She knew that she'd better nip that in the bud right away. This was real life and not some romantic fantasy where she was going to live happily ever after with a dashing billionaire bull rider. She wasn't Cinderella, and he wasn't her prince. He was facing a murder charge, for crying out loud.

Bowie hadn't seemed thrilled by the prospect of fatherhood, but then she'd hardly expected him to be happy about having a surprise child with a woman he barely knew. At least he hadn't called her a liar or demanded that she have an abortion.

His silence spoke volumes though. He hadn't asked to play a role in the baby's life. He hadn't offered to be there for her, except as financial provider, a role that she would never consider letting him play.

Lucy refilled the bucket. She was strangely calm. Whatever life threw at her, she knew she could take it. She and her baby were going to be fine.

Pregnant. A baby. A lifetime of responsibility. Bowie had always congratulated himself on not falling into this trap before now. He'd made mistakes in the past but had always gotten lucky. Now apparently his luck had run out.

Was it possible that Lucy had trapped him intentionally? She said she didn't know who he was, but that could have been an act.

No, that was impossible. He should be ashamed for even thinking it. She hadn't come after him, he'd approached her. And it was his fault for not being more careful with the condom.

Lucy had disappeared out of sight. Bowie felt a fierce urge to head for the hills in a cloud of dust.

He needed time to think.

Walking quickly and quietly, he entered the house. He retrieved his bag and found a piece of paper and a pen.

He had no idea what to write.

"Dear Lucy, I'm sorry about what happened. I promise I'll support you and the baby. I'm pretty freaked out right now and I need time to think." Honesty was the best policy. He signed it simply "Bowie."

Then he grabbed his bag, slipped out of the house, and gunned his car down the driveway as fast as he could.

Bowie forced himself to slow down as he reached a stretch of highway that was known for frequent traffic stops. He didn't need to run afoul of the speed laws now that he was already accused of murder.

Was the sky falling? He was facing decades in prison, and now a woman he barely knew was expecting his baby. What could happen next?

He gritted his teeth and reminded himself to focus on the road. At a time like this he needed family. Since Jesse was out of town looking at horses, and his brother Shane lived at the main West ranch with his dad—and was just as likely to disapprove of everything he said or did—he was going to have to drive up to his brother Daniel's mountain hideaway.

Daniel insisted that it was a hill, not a mountain, but it sure felt like a high peak when you tried to navigate his winding, poorly maintained road. He finally made it to the top, grateful for his custom truck suspension. His brother had also inherited his property when their mom died, and he rattled around alone in the nineteenth-century "log cabin" mansion built by the original owners.

Bowie approached the tall double doors and banged with his fist. "Dan, it's Bowie, open up!"

"Over here," called a voice from the trees to his left. "Chopping wood."

Bowie chuckled. Daniel was the Grizzly Adams of the family. More money than he could spend in a lifetime and liked to do everything the hard way.

Daniel looked up from his chopping, sweat dampening his black hair, and frowned. "Bowie? What are you doing here?"

"What kind of a welcome is that? I swear those wolves of yours have more manners than you do."

"Aren't you supposed to stay within a fifty-mile radius of Austin? I'm almost twice that."

"What's a mile or two when you're out here in the wilderness? Besides, it's an emergency."

Daniel put down his axe. "I could have come to you. What's going on?"

"You'd come off your mountain for me? I am touched." He attempted a smile. "But, yeah. Something strange happened." He didn't even know how to say it. His brother wasn't the type to have a one-night stand with a woman.

"Did the police find some evidence?"

"Nothing like that. Something totally different. I met this girl…a really nice girl." He inhaled sharply and shoved a hand through his hair. "And now she's pregnant."

Daniel stood up to his full height, which was impressive even to Bowie. "And you're sure it's yours?"

Bowie was embarrassed that he'd asked himself the same question. "She's not the type to sleep around." Bowie rubbed a hand over his face. "She's caring, she's kind, she runs a horse farm all by herself—I'm not kidding, she does all the work, and there are more than twenty horses there. She's a real person, Dan, not the kind of good-time girl I usually go for."

Dan's gray eyes looked thoughtful "Maybe it's a sign."

"A sign of what?" His brother could be infuriatingly enigmatic.

"That it's time for you to stop riding the wild wind and settle down."

"No, there's no way it could work out between me and her."

"Why not?" Daniel leaned on his axe.

"Because I'm me, Dan. I've never dated anyone longer than a few months. As soon as talk of commitment comes up my first and only instinct is to make like the Roadrunner. I'm happiest when I'm on the go, moving, traveling from place to place. I can't settle down, ever." He shoved a hand through his hair. "And the finals are coming up. I'll be traveling and riding in a different town every week between now and then."

"Unless the law has other plans for you." Daniel propped his axe against a neatly stacked pile of wood. "You've been charged with murder. It sounds to me like the universe is doing its best to put the brakes on your freewheeling lifestyle, and maybe you'd better start listening."

Listening to what? Daniel probably meant the trees or the river or maybe even the wolves he spent so much time with. Bowie glanced around to see if any of his furry familiars were lurking nearby. He could mount the craziest bull in all of Texas, but he still found wild animals unpredictable and alarming. "And you're one to talk. When was the last time you even went on a date?"

"What kind of woman would want to live out here in the woods?"

"See? You're no better than I am. You know that your lifestyle is incompatible with having a family."

Daniel frowned and turned toward the house.

"Did I say the wrong thing?" His brother had never shown the slightest interest in settling down with anyone. "Hey, I'm sure there are plenty of women who'd love to live in the woods." He glanced around again. "Who think wolves are awesome. You should post yourself on one of those dating websites. Get yourself a mail-order bride."

"I should punch your lights out, that's what I should do." The glitter of humor in Daniel's gray eyes showed that he wasn't really mad. He led Bowie into the house, with its carved wood beams and massive stone fireplace. "Besides, it doesn't sound like it's working out too well for you. What are you going to do?"

"That's just it. I don't know. I told her I'd support the baby, but she said she doesn't want that."

"She wants something more." Daniel offered him a drink in a corked bottle.

"I suppose so. She wants me in the baby's life."

"You can do that."

"Can I? I haven't done such a great job of being a son. I've been at odds with Dad since the day I was born. I don't even know how to be a father." He pulled the cork out of the bottle and took a swig of the mysterious dark brown brew. He almost spit it out on the floor. "What the hell is this? Are you trying to poison me?"

Daniel frowned. "It's wine. I made it from the wild grapes in my woods."

Bowie laughed. "I've had a lot of wine in my time and none of it tasted anything like this. If you do ever get a date, buy her some wine from the store, okay?"

"It's a acquired taste. Try it again."

Bowie narrowed his eyes and took a measured sip. This time the brew came as less of a surprise and he could appreciate a burned-sugary richness to it. "Still not so great, bro. But at least you managed to get my mind off my problems for a minute."

"You like this girl, right?"

"Sure. I mean, I only just met her, but I enjoy spending time with her." Every time he thought about Lucy, the rush of desire now mingled with a jab of apprehension.

"So give it time. See where it goes."

"That was my plan, but we seem to have gone from zero to way past sixty in less than a minute and I think I have whiplash."

Daniel took a long swig of his own dark brew and nodded in appreciation. "Look at it this way. The worst thing that could happen is she has your baby and you have nothing to do with it, and you don't ever see her again. Right?"

Bowie rubbed his forehead. "Yeah. I suppose so."

"So anything that you can do to keep from heading down that dark road is a start. Be honest with her. Tell her you travel—she knows you're a bull rider, right?"

"Yes."

"So she won't be expecting you to settle down with her. At least not right away. But you can visit her when you're not at a show, and get to know her and just give it time."

Bowie nodded. Put that way the whole situation didn't seem so intimidating. "She might tell me to get lost."

"She told you about the baby. If she didn't want you around, she wouldn't have bothered."

"She might be regretting her decision. She told me, and I took off."

"You need to get back there."

Bowie drew in a breath. "I do." He already regretted his rash impulse to run. It was the coward's way out. He wouldn't run from a bull. He'd climb aboard and ride it, no matter how bumpy things got. "I'd better get going before this stuff gets to my brain." He put down his bottle of the fierce homebrew.

"You spent a lot of time driving for a few words of wisdom." Daniel lifted a brow. "Ever heard of the phone?"

"Like you ever answer your phone."

"You could leave a message. Okay. I admit I'm not great at staying in touch with the outside world. I'm glad you came to me." He walked over and wrapped his big hand around Bowie's arm and squeezed it awkwardly.

The warm gesture touched Bowie, who hugged his brother. "I appreciate you being willing to both listen and talk some sense into me."

"Any time." Daniel stepped back, probably relieved to put some distance between them again. "Besides, you might be surprised to find that you're more ready to settle down than you think."

Bowie shook his head. "This year I'm in a good position to win the world championship."

"Then go for it, but don't burn any bridges along your road to glory."

"I'm going to head back to Lucy right now and be straight with her."

Bowie got back into his truck and navigated his way down Daniel's mountain toward the main road. Back in Denton he stopped at the supermarket to buy a bunch of flowers. They had red long stemmed roses, but it seemed phony to give her those. They were such a traditional symbol of love, and that wasn't he and Lucy had, at least not yet.

He chose a bunch of spring wildflowers and five small, pink roses, and asked the man tending the flowers to incorporate them into the bouquet. It looked pretty.

Then he grabbed a bag of carrots for the horses. Lucy had a lot of horses. He filled his arms with the remaining bags of carrots and headed to the counter. Outside, he turned the air-conditioning up high in the car to keep the flowers fresh, and drove back up to Lucy's ranch.

Bowie felt oddly calm. He knew she'd be angry with him for walking out on her, but he was pretty sure she'd be glad to see him back. He hadn't even been gone that long. Just a few hours. Hopefully, she could forgive and forget and they could move forward.

As he pulled into the driveway of her ranch, Bowie saw Lucy carrying a saddle toward the arena. He lowered the window and leaned out and called out her name.

Lucy totally ignored him.

10

When Lucy had come out of the barn and found that Bowie was gone, she assumed he'd gone into the house for a moment. When she found his little note, scrawled on the back of her shopping list, she'd been stunned.

You shouldn't be surprised, she'd told herself. She knew it was a possibility that he'd want nothing to do with you or the baby. But still, to run away without a word like that, only a few minutes after the magical kiss they had shared, revealed that Bowie West was not a man she could count on.

It was flattering that he still found her attractive enough to kiss her, but that wasn't what she needed right now.

If he was going to be the kind of father who'd show up for a while when it was convenient, then take off at the first sign of trouble, she'd just as soon raise her child without him.

"Lucy!"

He was back. She heard Bowie call her name but she resisted the instinct to turn and look at him. She finished tightening Pepper's girth and put his bridle on, then led him to the arena.

She knew at least one person who had ridden right up until a couple of weeks before delivery, and she hoped she could do the same. This horse belonged to one of her clients who paid her for training rides twice a week, and she couldn't afford to lose the income.

"Lucy." Bowie now stood at the arena gate. Lucy kept Pepper walking briskly around the arena. As she came around near the gate, she urged Pepper into a trot and moved past Bowie.

Out of the corner of her eye she could see he was carrying something that looked suspiciously like a bunch of flowers.

Why had he come back? He must be sorry for the way he'd run off. Had he come to apologize? Lucy couldn't help being curious. But she was still angry.

Very, very angry.

She coaxed Pepper into a canter and circled around the arena, picking up speed. As she cantered past Bowie she caught another glimpse of him. It was a bunch of flowers. And he had an armful of something orange.

No one had ever given her flowers before. What a shame that it wasn't a romantic moment that she could enjoy. She supposed that flowers were probably more often given as an apology than as a spontaneous romantic gesture.

She cantered around the arena again, deliberately avoiding looking toward the gate, though she was dying to get a glimpse of Bowie's expression. Would it be cocky self-assurance, to match the flirtatious gesture of the flowers? Or perhaps contrition and a desire to make amends.

Either way it didn't matter. Bowie West had shown

his true colors, and she knew she was better off without him.

Lucy took Pepper back to a trot and did a few serpentines back and forth across the arena, focusing on getting Pepper to bend nicely. He was coming along well and would be a nice dressage prospect.

As she dismounted Lucy wondered if she should lead her horse out of the gate at the far end of the arena, or if she should go and confront Bowie. She was being very rude to him. Was she testing him to see if he would go away and leave again?

She led her horse out the far gate and toward the barn. She could hear Bowie following her. As she put Pepper on the crossties, he caught up with her.

"Lucy, I'm sorry about the way I ran off this morning."

Lucy removed the bridle and hung it over her shoulder.

"There's no excuse for it. I cracked, I don't know what I was thinking."

She didn't look at his face, but she heard the edge in his voice. She was starting to feel a little guilty for ignoring him. But why? This jerk had run away moments after she'd told him they were having a baby.

She undid the cinch and lifted the saddle off Pepper's back.

Bowie put down the things he was carrying in the barn aisle.

"Here, let me take that. You shouldn't be carrying anything heavy."

"I'll be fine," said Lucy, as she steered past Bowie and latched the stall, keeping her eyes on the tack room at the end of the aisle.

"I can see why you don't want to talk to me, Lucy. I don't deserve it. What kind of an asshole would run out on a woman who just told him she's having his baby?"

Exactly.

"I don't have anything to say in my defense. I can't make any excuses for what I did. But I'll make you a promise. I'll never, ever, run out on you again. I don't care what happens. If you have to see me yell or curse or cry, I'll do it right in front of you. I promise you that I'll never turn my back on you again."

Bowie had followed her down to the tack room and stood in the doorway while she replaced the saddle and pad.

Lucy was touched by what he said. But then he was a famous bull rider with hordes of fans. He knew how to work women. That was written all over his handsome face, which she still hadn't dared to look at. He probably knew just what to say to make her think he could change.

Lucy turned and headed toward the door. Bowie filled the doorframe, and as she approached him Lucy had no choice but to look into his face. He was staring directly at her, and the look in his eyes made her heart begin to pound in her chest. The piratical glitter was gone from his eyes, and instead they shone with something quite different. Wariness but also...hope.

She swallowed hard.

"Please, Lucy, give me a chance to prove that I can be there for you."

"This is not some competition, Bowie," said Lucy, hot anger rising in her and spewing out through her mouth, "this is not some rodeo where you win a prize for sticking with it until the bell rings. This is my life. I'm having a baby, and that baby is going to need stability. I don't want to be your proving ground."

She pushed past him out into the aisle and glanced at the stuff that Bowie had placed on the floor there. The bunch of flowers looked pretty pathetic lying there on the floor. And there were about eight bags of carrots.

Carrots? Lucy paused.

"I brought the carrots for the horses."

"Why?"

"I don't know, I guess I figured I'd try and butter them up too, see if they could talk you into forgiving me."

Lucy couldn't help a slight smile playing across her lips. She turned to look at Bowie. "You'd better pick them up then. They're not going to do much good lying on the floor."

Bowie retrieved the carrots and the bunch of flowers. The soft buds and delicate sprays of flowers looked comically out of place in the dusty half-light of the barn aisle. Bowie didn't attempt to give it to her.

"I guess I'll feed this to the horses too," he said, looking at the bouquet. "They seem pretty cheesy, given the situation."

"No one's ever bought me flowers before." It just came out. Lucy bit her lip as if she could stop the words after they had left her mouth.

"I'd like to give you flowers, Lucy, but not these ones. I hope you'll give me a chance to give you flowers that aren't an apology for something I've done wrong. You deserve better."

Lucy took a deep breath. "Listen, Bowie, I told you about the baby because you are the father, biologically. I'd like my child to know his father. I'm not asking for anything more than that. I'm not looking to trap you into anything, I don't want to marry you, I don't want money, but I would like you to acknowledge your child and be there for him or her in some capacity.

"I'm sorry that this had to happen when you already have enough troubles to worry about. That's why I didn't tell you right away. When you arrived yesterday I couldn't bear to add another load to your burden.

"I'm sorry that we kissed, I hadn't meant that to happen. And I'm sorry I told you so bluntly, but I didn't know any other way."

"I'm not sorry that we kissed."

Bowie looked at Lucy. He stood tall and straight, his arms filled with his peace offerings, his head held erect in an attitude of defiance. She knew he was hurting, just as she was. It was a terrible shock to suddenly be responsible for a living being.

She felt a powerful urge to reach out to him, to try and bridge the distance that had sprung up between them since she made her announcement. But she kept her head, which told her that listening to her heart could only lead to that same heart being crushed and broken.

He might want to kiss her now, but what could it possibly lead to?

Was he going to be there for the 4 a.m. feedings she'd heard friends complaining about? Was he going to comfort a crying baby, or calm a hysterical toddler? Not likely. He'd probably be on the road between rodeos.

She straightened her shoulders. "Let's not pretend

there's something between us that just isn't there. I'd like us to try and be friends, so let's start again. Let's approach the situation as adults."

Bowie nodded slowly. "Okay."

Lucy felt a little twinge of disappointment. Of course Bowie wasn't in any position to argue with her. A few minutes ago she'd been ready to throw him off the ranch and never see him again.

"I have to feed the horses and make sure they all have water before turning in for the night."

"Let me do it, Lucy. I don't want you to overexert yourself."

I'd better get used to exerting myself while pregnant. He certainly wasn't going to be there every morning and night to do her work for her.

"Why don't you unwrap some of those carrots and give them to the horses? They could use a treat. And we'll put the flowers in water. They'll brighten up the kitchen, no sense wasting them."

The rumble of distant thunder made her look up at the sky, where dark purple clouds deepened the looming dusk. A sudden flash of lightning made her jump. "On second thought, we'll save the carrots for another time. I need to get everyone fed."

"At least let me help."

"If you insist." She couldn't stop a smile sneaking over her mouth. His willingness to help was endearing. "You can load the hay onto the UTV while I top up their water. "

"Deal." Fat raindrops already speckled the ground around them, and the boom of thunder grew closer. "And we'd better hurry."

Lucy hummed to herself as she filled the big troughs to the brim, sneaking glances at Bowie's broad back as he heaved bales of hay into the bed of the UTV.

Would he stay the night? She felt bad that he didn't get any sleep last night. Dancer had recovered fully and was happily grazing in her pasture. She had to give him credit for how much effort he'd put into helping her through the night.

"Six is enough," she called as she walked toward him. "We'll spread them out so everyone gets a chance. Three for the mares and three for the geldings."

And damn he looked good in those faded jeans and that soft checked shirt. *Lucy!* She'd been a fool to kiss him this morning and get him all excited before she dropped her baby bomb on him. They had a lot to work out, and getting steamy had only complicated things.

Bowie helped her spread the hay out in the paddocks, and she introduced him to the horses and told him some of their quirks and talents. It was fun sharing the daily chores with someone for a change, especially as the drizzle became more persistent.

"Can't complain too much about the rain. It's been dry lately. The grass could use a soaking." She took a deep breath. "Do you want to stay the night? This time you might actually get to sleep. In the spare room," she added hastily. She didn't want him to think she was trying to seduce or trap him into anything now he knew she was pregnant.

"I'd like that." His green eyes flashed the teeniest hint of triumph. He must be pleased with himself for getting on her good side again.

Which he had. He had a lot of charm, and she'd have to watch out for that!

By the time they'd spread the last bale the rain was heavy and insistent and they sped for the house and ran inside, dripping. She insisted that he shower first, and he had to run back out to his truck to retrieve his bag which he'd taken with him when he skipped out earlier.

She teased him for that, too. It was oddly easy to be with him now that the secret was out and she didn't have anything to hide. At least she had a chance to get to know him a little before he headed back out into the big wide world where the murder accusations and his rodeo career called to him.

They made dinner together—shrimp and a salad—and made careful conversation around impersonal topics like movies they liked and bands they'd seen live. It was like a first date—except they were far too wary to think about anything as racy as kissing or holding hands. There was too much at stake.

The storm still raged as they cleared the dishes. "I'd better go out and check on the horses. There are two of them in a small paddock near the hill that can take on some water. Nothing dangerous, but I don't like them standing ankle deep in it. I can bring them into the barn."

"I'm coming, too."

She liked that he didn't try to dissuade her from going outside. He knew that she took her responsibilities seriously. They jumped in the wet UTV and drove to the paddock, where, sure enough, a sheen of rain-pitted water covered half the grass. She grabbed the two halters from the gate and headed out across the high ground, where the horses sheltered under a spreading oak. Before she got there, Bowie joined her, took one of the halters, and deftly haltered the larger of the two horses. Without a word, he followed her into the barn and she showed him which stall to put his horse in.

She sighed as she hung the halter outside the stall. Some things really were easier with two people. These horses belonged to one of her boarders who didn't come often and they weren't too well trained. She might be still struggling to get the second halter on while the first horse danced about if she was by herself.

"Thanks, Bowie." She meant it sincerely.

"You're welcome." That victorious gleam in his eyes should have annoyed her, but instead it warmed her heart.

"I guess we should turn in now." She turned for the house, wondering if maybe—just maybe—a kiss wouldn't be such a completely terrible idea. Then a flash of lightning illuminated the barn aisle and a huge crash shook the building.

11

Lucy froze. "What the heck was that?"

"Sounds like lightning struck something real close." Bowie was already halfway down the aisle. "It's a tree. It's down across your driveway."

"Oh, no." The beautiful old oak trees on the property were like close friends to her. She reached his side to see one of them split almost in half, with a huge branch more than a foot across stretching across the drive leading up to the barn and—"It's on the fence." The end of the branch had broken two rails in the gelding paddock. "I need to fix it before they find the hole and escape. One time a two-year-old ran through a fence during a storm and half of the geldings got loose before I found out. I was out all afternoon rounding them up with buckets of grain."

"You got a hammer, nails, and spare boards?"

"Right in here." She led the way into the tack room, where she kept emergency supplies on hand. Bowie didn't even ask, he just grabbed them and headed out into the rain. He nailed the boards up with the tree still in place. Less than five minutes after the lighting strike the problem was solved.

She'd probably still be trying to heave two twelve-foot-long boards down the rainy driveway if she was alone.

"In the morning I'll cut up the tree, but for now they're safe. Do you have a chainsaw?"

She nodded. She'd bought it and been too nervous to use it after reading all the warnings about kickback. "I'm not mad at you anymore, Bowie. I think you're pretty awesome."

"Aw, shucks," he joked. "I'm just glad I'm here to help."

Me, too.

Though of course it would hurt all the more when he finally left and she was back on her own again, this time with a needy baby to look after.

She showed him to his room and didn't stand still long enough for him to get any ideas about kissing her. Not that he'd even want to. "The shower's in there and there's a clean towel on the rack. Take your time. I'll use it when you're done." Her small house had only one bathroom. As a wealthy heir, not to mention a champion rodeo star, he was probably used to luxury accommodations.

"Thanks, Lucy. See you in the morning."

See? He didn't even try to sweet-talk her into bed. No doubt her pregnant state had scared him off. As well it might. Pregnant women were often only interested in one thing—marriage. And rolling stone Bowie West was not likely to be too excited about that.

The next morning she was awakened by the sound of a chainsaw outside her window. She looked out to see Bowie already cutting the big branches off the fallen tree. How did he even find the chainsaw? And put gas in it?

He was frighteningly competent.

She got dressed and hurried downstairs. "You're a miracle worker," she shouted, as she drew close.

He shut off the saw. "What?"

"I said—never mind. How did you find the chainsaw?"

"I just hunted around in the kinds of places a chainsaw might like to hide." His rakish grin disarmed her. She should probably be peeved that a virtual stranger was rifling through her possessions—even she couldn't remember where she'd left it, probably the old toolshed she rarely used—but how could she be mad when he'd already cleared her blocked driveway?

"I figured you'd want the driveway usable before any of your boarders show up to ride."

"You're a pretty cool guy, Bowie."

"So they tell me." He winked, gunned the chainsaw engine, and got back to cutting up the tree.

Lucy shook her head and sighed.

He didn't stop until it was all done and the chunks of tree loaded into his truck and moved to the end of the driveway for trash pickup or stacked behind the barn for firewood. She was really touched by him doing so much to help when someone with his unlimited funds would probably just call in a crew if it was his place. She was grateful that he didn't put her in an awkward position by suggesting that, since she couldn't afford it and wouldn't want to accept charity in the form of him paying for it.

There was something altogether different about him doing the work himself, though. His strength, determination and persistent good cheer were impressive—and very sexy.

She was running electric tape to temporarily divide a paddock when he strode over and declared that he was finished.

"You have no idea how much I appreciate it. You must be exhausted."

"Not even slightly. Sawing up wood is my idea of a good time. What are you doing?"

"Cross-fencing these paddocks so I can move more horses in. The ones at the base of the hill always flood after a big storm. The water keeps coming out of that hill for days so I need to move the horses for a week or so."

"You should put in drainage along the base of the hill to take the water off somewhere else. You could drain it right down to that creek along the far side of those paddocks."

"I'd love to, but I don't own that land. I even tried writing to them offering to buy that strip of it but never heard back."

"Who owns it?"

"Some faceless corporation. They're listed on the tax records as WEG Enterprises with an address in Austin. They didn't even acknowledge my letter."

Bowie's face changed while she was talking. "WEG? Was the address Twelve Acre Circle?"

Lucy frowned. "Yes. I think it was. Do you know them?"

"I am them. WEG is the West Enterprises Group." Light danced in his eyes. "I guess I didn't realize my land stretched all the way back here. I've had it leased out to an old cattleman for years, and he maintains all the fence and keeps the brush under control so I don't have to think about it."

Lucy blinked, open-mouthed but speechless. Was

this good or bad? It could solve all her problems, or—if things went sour between them—screw her over completely.

"I have an administrator who deals with most of my correspondence, and I never saw it. I apologize for behaving like a faceless corporation." He obviously saw some humor in the situation. She wasn't so sure.

"You're my next-door neighbor?"

"Yep. And I clearly have a drainage problem on my land that's causing trouble for you so I'm going to get it fixed. A phone call, a backhoe, and some drain tile and your land will be so dry you'll have to put out sprinklers."

She laughed. It was impossible not to since he was so clearly pleased with the idea. Then she sobered. "It's not your problem, it's mine."

"It isn't anyone's problem now." He was already dialing a number and proceeded to have a conversation with someone called Bender, who apparently agreed to show up with the equipment that afternoon. "I'll help you bring the horses over here so they're not spooked by the equipment. He's fast and neat. You'll like the results."

She stood there, speechless for a moment. "You own that whole tract, all the way out to the main highway?"

He nodded. "I should be ashamed of myself for ignoring it for so long. I've just been too focused on my rodeo career and traveling all the time. It's the five thousand acres I told you about, which I inherited when my mom died."

"Wow." She'd worked so hard to scrape and save for her measly five acres. But she wasn't going to be bitter about it. "Lucky you. It's a beautiful piece of land. Is there a house on it?"

"No. There was once, but it burned down. Right now there's just a big old barn that the farmer uses for hay storage. I'll take you on a tour of the place some time."

"I'd like that." Somehow Bowie owning a small empire right next to her barn made him even more intimidating and unavailable. "Some of those live oaks must be hundreds of years old."

"It's been in my family since before Texas was a thing. My dad asked me to sell it back to him, but I like the idea of settling down there one day when I'm old and gray."

Lucy nodded, her mind spinning. Of course Bowie wasn't going to settle down any time before that. At least not if he could help it.

Still, he helped her move the six horses in the flooded paddocks. Bender showed up and they walked all along the base of the hill with him, making plans and watching him start work with the backhoe he'd brought on a big trailer.

"I can't believe it's so late already." It was nearly four in the afternoon. "I'm going to bring Rapunzel here in to ride." The pretty palomino was named for her long, blonde mane. "Her owner just had a baby so she hasn't ridden her in a while and I'm supposed to keep her fit."

"Should you be riding?" Bowie cocked his head, suddenly thoughtful.

"The doctor wasn't crazy about the idea, but she also said that she'd plenty of patients who did, so it was up to me if I wanted to take the risk. The riding itself is fine. It's the falling off that's a problem."

"When did you last fall off?"

"A long time ago."

"Then I think I'll let you ride a little. No jumping or crazy galloping on the trails, though."

"You'll *let* me ride?" Her hackles shot up.

Bowie nodded, "For now, anyway, but you'd better be careful—our baby's depending on you."

Her annoyance faded immediately. He not only acknowledged and accepted their baby, he was already concerned about him or her. That touched her somewhere tender inside.

"Have you figured out which room is going to be the baby's?" Bowie asked. "I'd be happy to paint it or do anything else you need."

"Hmm, I hadn't thought about it yet." She wasn't even out of the first month yet. According to one pregnancy site she'd read on the Internet, most people didn't even tell anyone about their pregnancy at this point, let alone redecorate their house for the baby. "There's still more than eight months to worry about that stuff."

"Do you want to find out the gender of the baby?" he asked.

Lucy shrugged, "Not really, it doesn't matter to me either way. Are you curious?"

"A little, but it'll be nice to have it be a surprise, the old fashioned way. Guess I can paint the room yellow or something."

Lucy was staring at Bowie wide-eyed. He'd pulled a Swiss Army knife from his pocket and was tightening the screw that held a crosstie ring in place.

"Have you thought about names?" he asked, before looking up.

Lucy shook her head, "No, not at all." Bowie

suddenly seemed to be way ahead of her when it came to planning for their child's future. She was just trying to get through each day of her pregnancy. "It feels so odd to get to choose the name of another person, something that they'll carry though their whole life."

"I know," Bowie grinned. "I have no idea how I ended up being called Bowie. Maybe my mom was listening to a David Bowie album or something."

"It suits you. It's a knife, isn't it? A bowie knife."

"Yep, and some people say I have sharp edges."

"Definitely." She looked at his biceps as he turned the tool. Hard edges, Bowie had them all over. Everything about him was hard, rugged, built to go the distance.

Lucy could feel heat rising inside her. Why did Bowie have to be so damned attractive? He folded up his knife then turned and caught her looking at him. He knocked a stray wisp of hair out of his eyes.

"That ring had worked loose. I'll check them and tighten them all up."

Lucy chuckled while she groomed Rapunzel. "Don't work too hard. Feel free to ride the horses, too."

"Maybe I'll have another ride on Wonder. I like that horse."

"Go for it."

"And where's the nearest supermarket? I want to buy some food."

"You don't have to do that."

"I know, but I want to. I love to cook and I'm pretty good at it."

He cooked as well? Maybe this whole thing was an elaborate anxiety dream and she was about to wake up—alone. But until then... "There's a supermarket near the highway exit. You can't miss it."

After he left, Lucy chatted with a couple of the barn clients who were there to ride. She'd noticed them looking curiously at Bowie as he drove off, but neither of them asked about him and she didn't say anything. What would she have said if they did? *Oh, he's just a champion bull rider and I'm carrying his baby so he's helping out with some chores.* The thought made her laugh. At least she still had her sense of humor.

Bowie wasn't back when she'd finished with the evening barn chores, so she decided to take a long, hot shower and spruce herself up a bit. Bowie had seen her looking her absolute worst for the last couple of days. There was no harm in trying to look presentable for a change.

As the hot water coursed over her body, she let herself enjoy the pure sensual pleasure of it. Her mind wandered back to the nights she and Bowie had spent together at Singing Pines, one out under the stars, where she slept with Bowie's hand resting on her waist, and the other in her bed, the sheets warmed and scented with sex.

She let out a long sigh. Bowie had not said anything about the kiss that had taken them both by surprise before she'd told him about the pregnancy. No doubt he regretted it, as he must regret the encounter at Singing Pines that had gotten him tangled up—permanently—in her life.

As she dried herself with the towel and surveyed the clothes in her closet, Lucy caught sight of the fateful black dress that had started all this trouble. She chuckled at the thought of what Bowie's face would do if she greeted him at the door in it. He certainly was attracted to her when she wore it. And if she wasn't mistaken he was attracted to her when she wasn't wearing it.

But she couldn't let a little healthy male lust lure her into thinking that there might a romantic future between her and Bowie. He probably looked at a lot of women that way. He was probably looking at someone like that right now, as he pushed a cart down the supermarket aisle.

He probably wasn't even at the supermarket. He'd been gone for more than two hours. Maybe he'd decided to skip town—again.

But just in case...Lucy put on some well-fitting jeans and a black blouse. She left three buttons undone, just for the fun of seeing Bowie try to keep his eyes off her cleavage. *Not bad, cowgirl,* she thought as she looked in the mirror.

The sound of his car in the driveway lifted her spirits. Still, she stayed upstairs in her bedroom while she heard Bowie unpack the groceries. It was probably a good idea to give him a little space. She'd piled a lot on his head when he already had his legal troubles to worry about.

She grinned and her heart started to race as she heard him come pounding upstairs, but he headed into the bathroom and she heard the shower running. Visions of his hard, naked body glistening with water were definitely a torment. She stayed firmly put until she was pretty sure she'd heard him get dressed again.

Then he bounded back downstairs. It was like having a teenage boy in the house. Bowie never went anywhere at a walk. She wouldn't be at all surprised to see him sliding down the banisters.

Pots and pans clattered in the kitchen, and she heard the sound of running water and the thunk of a knife slicing through vegetables.

Let's go see what he's up to. She looked down at her belly. *Your dad.* She shook her head. It still didn't sound right. She supposed she would get used to the idea eventually.

12

"Hey, Lucy," Bowie turned his head toward her as she came down the stairs. He did a double take and grinned as he took in her ensemble. "You look nice."

"Thanks." That was all she was able to say, as her mind took in the sight of Bowie's lithe, tanned body dressed only a pair of black athletic shorts. His hair was wet and uncombed, tumbling forward as he focused on the food he was preparing.

Lucy's pulse accelerated as she watched. The muscles in his arms flexed as he chopped an onion and sprinkled it into hot oil. Two pots were already steaming away on the stove.

"Can I help you with something?" Her voice sounded embarrassingly breathless.

"You could slice up these green beans for me."

Lucy moved toward him, watching the tiger dance on his back as he chopped another onion. Offering to help was probably a mistake. Now she was going to have to stand much too close to him.

The small countertop was cluttered with opened cans of coconut milk, bowls of chopped meat, and exotic spices.

"What are you making?"

"A few different things. I decided to go

Indonesian tonight. Your local supermarket has a pretty good selection of spices and you can always find good hot chiles in Texas."

He smiled at her and her heart fluttered beneath her unbuttoned blouse. He handed her a colander full of freshly rinsed green beans.

"Just slice them longways, like this." His fingers moved deftly as he demonstrated the correct technique.

"Where did you learn to cook Indonesian food?"

"In Indonesia, of course."

"Of course." She sliced the green beans diagonally, the way Bowie had showed her. He stood right next to her, stirring the onions and lifting the lids to check on the dishes on the stove.

She could smell the soap on his skin, mingled with his own spicy male scent. With its heady brew of sautéing onions, fragrant coconut milk and powdered chilies, the air in the kitchen was intoxicating.

Bowie added meat to a sizzling pan on the stove, his movements deft and precise, not what you'd expect from the bouncing teenager she'd compared him to earlier.

He stirred, measured spices and poured in coconut milk with perfect concentration while Lucy struggled to keep her mind on the beans. It would be embarrassing to sever an artery while performing such a simple task.

She was relieved when she was done and could step back a little. The pans weren't the only things that were steaming. Bowie was obviously getting hot in the warm kitchen and a tiny trickle of sweat ran down the back of his neck and traced a delicate line down his back, following the hollow of his spine.

It must have tickled him as he paused in his task and reached a hand behind him to scratch his back, dipping his fingers just inside the waistband of his shorts.

Lucy took a deep breath and wiped a few tiny beads of dew from her temples. Was he wearing only shorts just to torment her?

She tried to busy herself setting the table.

"It'll be ready in a few minutes," he said. "Could you pour us some water to drink?"

"Sure." She was going to need some water to cool off even before eating any spicy food. "You don't have to drink water on my account though. Go ahead and have a beer if you want to."

"No, that's okay. Water's fine."

"Do you want me to get you some clothes?" Lucy tried to sound casual. She wasn't sure she'd be able to keep a straight face if she'd to sit across the table from a shirtless Bowie.

"I've used up all my clean clothes. I'm fine, really."

"I could lend you a T-shirt." *Please, please, please!*

"No, I'm okay." Then he turned to her. "Unless it bothers you. I guess it's a bit rude to wander around your house like I'm in my own home."

"Oh, no, it's fine, great. Please, make yourself at home, as I said when you arrived." She hoped her hand gestures weren't too extravagant. She pushed her hair back off her forehead. She was feeling overheated out of all proportion to the actual temperature of the kitchen.

Bowie seemed to know her kitchen better than she did as he removed dishes and bowls from the cabinets and began to spoon the cooked food into them. Lucy helped him carry the steaming plates over to the table.

"The main dishes are chicken in coconut milk and this dry beef curry, then the rest are side dishes. This is prawn sambal, green bean sambal, some spiced coconut with peanuts, to sprinkle on top if you want, fried bananas, and of course, rice."

Bowie looked pleased with himself as he surveyed the laden table.

"The two of us are going to eat all of this?"

"The three of us are, yes." He raised his eyebrows and smiled. "Bon appetit." He raised his glass of water and Lucy clinked hers against it.

The food was sensational—fragrant, filling, and altogether a sensual dining experience.

Bowie chatted about his travels in Indonesia and how he'd learned the recipes while living with a family there. His eyes didn't go anywhere near her cleavage. He talked earnestly, eating and drinking, as if he were with an old pal.

Lucy tried to keep her eyes on his face, but every now and then, when he was cutting up a mouthful or helping himself to more rice, she snuck a look down at his torso, where a thin sprinkling of gold hairs ornamented the dark skin of his chest.

Her whole body was tingling in a most disconcerting way. She'd read that pregnancy dramatically increased the blood flow in her body, forging thousands of new blood vessels. Apparently, all those new vessels were carrying raging hormones to the farthest corners of her body.

She tried to focus on what Bowie was saying, something about building a hut out of banana leaves, but her mind kept losing focus as her eyes wandered over the planes of his face, his sensual mouth, his high cheekbones, his dark jade eyes.

"Don't you think so?" he said, forking some rice into his mouth. Lucy stared open mouthed for a second. "You haven't been listening to me," said Bowie, tilting his head. The corners of his mouth curled up slightly. "You're probably tired. Shall we go rest on the sofa and watch some TV?"

"Okay," said Lucy tonelessly. At least then she wouldn't have to be sitting directly opposite him, being taunted by the swells and hollows of his muscled physique while the flavors of his cooking danced on her palate.

They carried the dishes into the kitchen and put them in the dishwasher. Try as she might, Lucy just couldn't seem to keep her eyes from wandering over Bowie's unclothed body.

As he bent over the dishwasher, arranging cutlery in the tray, her eyes traced the curve of his spine. He turned suddenly, with a question on his lips, and caught her eyes planted firmly on his backside.

"What are you looking at?" he teased. She saw a glimmer of mischief in his gaze. Lucy felt a dark blush rising up from beneath her blouse, and Bowie noticed it too. "Red suits you." He chuckled and finished arranging the silverware.

Once Bowie noticed Lucy admiring him so unguardedly, something shifted in the atmosphere.

Bowie reached the sofa first and stretched himself along its length, catlike, one leg extended and the other bent, foot on the floor. "I don't know if there's room for both of us," he teased. Aside from a wooden chair there was no other furniture to sit on.

"But you can probably squeeze in here," he patted the flowered sofa cushion next to his bare chest.

Lucy switched on the television and carefully

seated herself at the far end of the sofa, lifting his extended leg, then resettling it on her lap. His knee was rather scarred.

"What do you want to watch?" she asked.

"Anything, whatever you want. I don't watch TV much so it's all good."

"I don't watch it much either." There was a tennis game on and Lucy lingered on that channel, watching the players dancing back and forth at their baselines.

The station went to a commercial break, and Lucy leaned over to grab the remote so she could change the channel when Bowie leaned forward and grabbed her hand. She looked up at his face, and his eyes were firmly fixed on her breasts, which angled toward him.

"Hold on a minute, I'm enjoying the view."

Lucy ripped her arm away from him. She supposed she should probably slap his face or something, but she laughed instead.

Bowie's eyes were dark with desire as he looked at her. Her body responded with a surge of heat below her belly button. Then his mouth closed hungrily over hers.

Heat flashed through her as his tongue touched hers. His hand roved over her belly and up to her breast, gently cupping its weight and stroking over the hardened nipple.

Lucy let out an involuntary gasp as Bowie's hand pulled back her bra and rubbed her nipple with his palm. He lowered his mouth to her breast and sucked until she moaned.

When he raised his face to her, his eyes were dark with passion. He kissed her harder, holding her close and rubbing his hands up and down her back, touching her hips, her waist, her shoulders, warming her and making her body melt into his.

His shorts bulged with evidence of his need for her. Gingerly she reached out a hand and touched the erection pressing against the black fabric. Bowie shuddered, convulsed with desire.

"Can we make love?" asked Bowie anxiously, his voice rough. "Did the doctor say it was okay?"

"Yes," replied Lucy, "yes, yes." She'd never felt so aroused in her life.

"I don't believe it. I didn't bring any condoms." Bowie looked horrorstruck.

"We don't need one. I'm already pregnant. Come here, quickly, please." Lucy's whole body ached for this man.

Hesitantly, Bowie unbuttoned Lucy's blouse and undressed her gently. His fingers tremble as he pulled down her panties, and lowered his mouth over her sex. She was already wet, her whole body throbbing with longing from the torment of watching Bowie's perfect physique moving, at ease, in her kitchen and her life.

Bowie sucked her greedily, as her hands played in his hair. The sensations building in her body were almost painful. She wanted Bowie inside her, now. She pulled him toward her and roughly pushed his shorts down and he sprang free.

Still kneeling on the floor, he thrust gently into her. She sank back into the sofa cushions, pulling him with her, her hips lifted to welcome him.

He arched over her, burying his face in her breasts as he pushed further into the continent of her body, moving slowly, on a voyage of tender exploration. Faster, slower, deeper, softer, in and out.

Lucy abandoned herself to the whirlwind of

sensation. She felt as if she were being lifted by a tornado and spun at warp speed through the universe, silver darts of light spinning through the air around her.

Her whole body was alive with the magic of Bowie's touch. She writhed and twisted under him as a wave of pulses rose within her. An explosion ricocheted through her and she heard gasps escaping her mouth, but she had no control over them.

She had no control over anything anymore. Waves of tension and release rocked her, robbing her of her senses. She heard Bowie groan and push deeper into her as his own climax ripped through him.

He collapsed onto her, his breath coming in short gasps. He wrapped his arms tightly around her and held her tight—so tight—their bodies pressing together in the intimacy of the moment.

They stayed like that, holding each other, as they both returned to consciousness.

"That was incredible," she murmured.

Bowie nodded, his green eyes wide with amazement. He kissed her softly on the lips. He eased himself gently out of her, his expression pained at having to depart from the warm, safe haven of her body.

Bowie went to clean up, and Lucy stretched herself out on the sofa. Her body felt perfect, warm and tingling with pleasure, each full curve exactly where it should be.

She could see Bowie enjoying the sight of her unfurled before him, like a Renaissance nude on a gilded chaise.

"You are a goddess," said Bowie. "Can I worship you?"

Lucy smiled. Bowie came and sat on the sofa beside her. His fingers warm and gentle, he followed the arch of her hips, stroking her sensuous curves like a sculptor admiring his own creation.

His fingers wandered over her waist and down to her belly, where they rested. He looked into her eyes. "What do you think our baby thought about all that?"

"It must have been a pretty wild ride." They both chuckled as Bowie's hand moved over her womb.

"When is your belly going to start to get big?" he asked, fingering her belly button.

"Not for a long time yet, from what I've read. Do you think it will bother you?"

"No," Bowie shook his head. His jade eyes were soft with wonder. "I think it's going to be glorious. I've newly awakened to the magic of full, rounded curves, and I just can't get enough." He leaned forward and kissed her belly.

"I have a confession to make," said Lucy. Bowie looked at her curiously. She wasn't sure why she needed to tell him, but she did. Still, her heart pounded while she said it. "I was a virgin when we met."

13

Bowie blinked. "You mean you never...?"

"Nope." Lucy held her breath. Would he be so shocked that he'd never see her the same way again?

"At Singing Pines, that was the first time?"

"Yes." It was an embarrassing confession, but she tried to be honest in all aspects of her life and keeping that secret would be another burden.

He did look shocked. "Jeez, I had no idea. I don't think I've ever even met a virgin before. Why didn't you say something at the time?"

"Would you still have made love to me?"

Bowie paused. "Probably not."

"That's why I didn't say anything. I wanted to be with you that night. It was a decision that I made." Then she quickly added. "But I certainly didn't mean to get pregnant." She hoped he didn't think she'd somehow planned it.

"It was my fault for not putting the condom on fast enough. Still, it's the start of a new adventure." He stroked her hair.

Bowie was doing a good job of putting a brave face on in this situation. She was sure any guy would be pretty freaked out. She wanted to ask more, to plan the future—as she lay in his arms any number of wonderful things seemed possible.

But she didn't want to scare him off, either.

Still, one question had been preying on her mind. "When's the next rodeo you need to ride in, to pursue the world title?"

"Next week. It's more than fifty miles from Austin, though, so I'll need permission to travel there. My lawyer is working on it."

"And you can stay here until then?"

He started to smile, then a wry expression crossed his face and darkened his eyes. "Unless the universe has other plans for me that I don't know about."

"I know what you mean." She sighed. "But I guess we just have to take life moment by moment right now."

He stroked her chin gently with his thumb. "I've lived my life eight seconds at a time so that sounds about right to me."

She rested her head on his chest. For now, he was hers. And their baby's. Next week? Who knew. Until then, she was going to enjoy Bowie and try to get to know him, but she also vowed to be sensible not let her heart get too tangled up in dreams of a future that might never happen.

Two days later, Lucy ran across the rain-soaked barnyard, trying to hold her slicker over her head, and ran headlong into Bowie, who dropped one of the two hay bales in his arms.

He dropped the other and grabbed her. "Sorry, Lucy, I couldn't see where I was going. I knew I should have left that last bale behind. Are you okay?"

"I thought you were supposed to sweep me off my feet, not knock me off them." She laughed, catching her breath. "Besides, I think I ran into you. What are you doing out here in the rain? I thought you were stacking the bales in the barn." He'd been so helpful over the last few days that it was getting ridiculous.

"The hay's getting low in the far paddock. I thought I'd top it up before we head inside and light up a fire to dry off."

"That sounds like the best idea I've heard all day. I'll get that last bale." Before he could protest she picked it up and strode across the gravel toward the paddocks—which were wonderfully dry even in this deluge. "The new ditch is working like a charm. Usually water would be pooling at the base of the hill and getting ready to run over into the paddocks. There's no water at all anywhere."

Bowie cut the baling twine and tossed the hay over the fence, where each pile was greeted eagerly by the assembled horses.

"Yes, it's working well." Rain poured down his face as he surveyed his handiwork proudly. "When it dries out I'll sow some grass seed, and these pastures will be as green as the ones on top of the hill."

"Well, I know better than anyone that you have a natural talent for sowing seed." Lucy peeked out at him from under the yellow hood of her slicker and saw his eyebrows lift in surprise.

"You're getting to have quite a mouth on you, young lady."

"You're just getting to know me better. You might not like me so much once all your illusions about innocent virgins have been dashed."

"Oddly enough, the more I learn about you the more I like you." He stepped forward, pushing her hood back off her head and letting the rain pour down over the cascading tendrils of her dark hair. "You're just full of my kind of surprises."

He slid his arms inside her raincoat and pulled her toward him. Warm rainwater ran into their mouths as they opened them to kiss. Steam rose gently from them into the damp air as they allowed their hands to roam over each other.

There wasn't anywhere she'd rather be than in Bowie West's arms. When he held her, she felt safe. She'd been alone so long that she was used to being tough enough to take on the world by herself. Now that she was getting a taste of what it was like to share your burdens and your joys with someone else she in danger of becoming addicted.

"I have an idea." He took her hand and turned toward the barn. "I don't think I've ever had a roll in real hay."

"I think you'll find it rather scratchy," said Lucy doubtfully. But then she'd never had a roll in real hay either. Rolling in the hay seemed to be pretty popular, so who was she to go against tradition?

It was pretty scratchy, particularly afterward when they were pulling bits of alfalfa out of their hair and underwear. But it was an adventure, the kind of adventure that Lucy didn't even know she'd been missing until it followed her home from vacation.

The adventure lasted four more days. On the fifth day Bowie headed into Austin for a hearing to discuss whether he could compete in the upcoming rodeo. He promised he'd call her as soon as it was done, and be back in time for dinner.

But he didn't come back.

Lucy carried her phone around all afternoon and

most of the night. It rang, sure enough, but it was never Bowie at the other end of the line. That evening she listened for the sound of his car in the driveway, but it never came.

As she sat on the sofa that night—alone—she couldn't help the doubts creeping around the edges of her consciousness.

While he was with her, at the ranch, Bowie had managed to convince himself that he was capable of a commitment. But perhaps once he was gone, back in his own element, with all the forces of his old life swirling around him, his thoughts and actions took him in different and more familiar directions.

As Lucy did the chores by herself, she realized how much she'd grown used to counting on him. Although she was still early in the first trimester, everything seemed to take more effort and tire her out fast. Bowie had been so quick to carry every bale of hay and empty every bucket while he was there.

Given the choice of a return to the ranch or a night out on the town with his old partying friends, perhaps the latter had held more appeal. She shouldn't be surprised really.

You might keep a tiger in a cage as long as the door is locked, but once you open that cage, don't expect the tiger to sit there quietly waiting for its next meal. That tiger will jump out the door and be gone.

The house, which had always been such a peaceful haven from the outside world, now seemed quiet and lonely without Bowie. There were no large boots cluttering the porch, the kitchen didn't smell of the strange food he liked to cook, there was no one to high-five when her favorite team won, and her bed looked cold and empty.

At ten o'clock she broke down and texted him just to ask how things were going.

No response.

By eleven she was desperate to talk to someone, so she picked up the phone to call Val, then realized that she'd been so wrapped up in Bowie during the past few days that she hadn't even told her best friend about her pregnancy.

There's no time like the present. That was her new motto, apparently. She dialed Val's number and sucked in a deep breath.

"Lucy, I was beginning to wonder what happened to you. If I hadn't been working such long hours this week I'd have come over and found out."

She decided to cut to the chase. "And I'm pregnant."

"No." It wasn't a question.

"Yes." She had to smile. "You think I'd make something like that up?"

"No." Through the silence she could picture Val trying to form words but abandoning each attempt.

Finally she couldn't stand it any longer. "I got pregnant that first time. I went to the doctor to get some real contraception, they did some routine tests, and voila."

"Congratulations! Or should I say that you have the worst luck in the world. You got pregnant your very first time."

"I'm still in shock about it, but I'm warming to the idea a little bit more every day."

"You told the handsome cowboy yet?"

"About that…" She told Val about their few magical days and how Bowie had failed to return from his day in court.

"You never look at the news, do you?"

"Uh, no." Fear crept up her spine. "Why?"

"New evidence turned up. He was arrested as soon as he arrived at the courthouse and bail has been rescinded."

"What kind of evidence?"

"They found some of the murder victim's possessions in his apartment." Val spoke quietly. "Did you know she was a hooker?"

"An exotic dancer," she protested. "But he didn't even know her. He'd never met her before."

Silence again. Did Bowie really have an affair with this woman? Possibly. He was no virgin. He'd probably dated a hundred women.

"Are you still there?" asked Val gently.

"I'm here. He didn't kill her, you know." The items could have been planted when the gun was stolen.

"Sweetie, I know you guys have become close very fast, but you still hardly know him."

It was true. But she knew one thing. "He couldn't possibly have killed her because he was sleeping with me when the murder happened."

"You're kidding."

"No. And he didn't have time to go over there, kill her and come back before morning. In fact we barely had time to sleep." She couldn't have slept that deeply, could she? Enough for him to leave and come back? She couldn't imagine that.

"Do the police know this?"

"I don't know. He didn't want to drag me into it. He was out on bail and seemed confident that the charges would be dropped." She drew in a deep breath. "But that was before he was arrested again.

128

He'd be a fool not to tell them now. Ugh, I need to talk to him. Why wouldn't he call me?"

"You can't just make phone calls in jail. They take your phone away."

Lucy felt terrible for not trusting him. "I'm going to vouch for him."

"Be careful, sweetie. There might be more to this—to him—than you know."

"I'm already in this up to my neck. I'm having his baby." She touched her belly, and strange feelings roamed through her. "And no matter what else he may have done, I know he didn't kill that girl."

14

The next morning Lucy scanned the local paper's website. There had been nothing there the previous night but it might have news on the case.

She found the item easily, with depressing pictures of the dead woman's personal effects: a bottle of deodorant, a well-used lipstick and some blue lace underwear. The kind of things you would leave at your lover's—or client's—house if you stayed the night regularly. Another blurry and flash-lit picture showed the woman—Terri Balboa—who was pretty in a hard-bitten sort of way. She was also forty-three years old, originally from Indiana, and had a string of aliases and a long history of vice convictions.

What Bowie did with her is none of my business. She tried to convince herself but wasn't entirely successful. He'd said from the beginning that he didn't know her—so if he did, then at the very least he'd lied to her. And how else would her possessions be at his apartment?

On the other hand, why wouldn't he have disposed of them at the first opportunity? If someone planted the murder weapon at the scene with his prints on it, then they could have planted her effects in his apartment.

Reading on she learned that due to Bowie's wealth and familiarity with international travel, the prosecutor had convinced the judge that no amount of bail would be adequate to keep Bowie West in the country. He had claimed to be at his brother's dude ranch but that he could not offer an alibi for that particular night. He'd said that he was alone in his room, and did not speak to anyone between dinner and departing the ranch the following morning.

Lucy grew numb with horror. Bowie had actually lied to the prosecutor to protect her. She knew he wanted to protect her, but his misguided chivalry could land him a long stretch behind bars.

Anger surged through her. She was done letting him "protect" her. She wasn't a delicate flower who needed protecting from anything. If he wouldn't save himself then she'd do it for him.

She contemplated calling the police with her information, but it dawned on her that Bowie could be accused of perjury for lying to the police in the first place, so she decided it would be safer for him if she approached his lawyer first.

The name of Bowie's lawyer was mentioned in the article, so she looked him up and called right away. When she said that she could provide an alibi for Bowie West, the receptionist put her right through to Bowie's attorney.

"Mr. Crane?"

"Speaking."

"My name is Lucy Neel. I was with Bowie West all night on the night of the murder and I'll be happy to say so in court."

"You were at Singing Pines ranch with him?"

"Yes, we met there and we spent the night

together in my room. There's no way he could have left without my knowledge."

"I appreciate your coming forward." Mr. Crane hesitated. "My client did tell me the same information but insisted that I not use it."

"Why?"

"He knows—as do I—that the prosecutor will try to prove you an unreliable witness and will probably attack your reputation. It could get really ugly. Frankly, you meeting Mr. West and sleeping with him within the space of three days is just the kind of thing that he will play up in court as he tries to discredit you and my client. If he is able to cast doubt on your reliability, then there will be no way of proving that my client did spend the night with you."

"But there is."

Lucy's heart was pounding. She felt so cheapened by what Mr. Crane had said. The testimony of a loose woman didn't count for much in a court of law. But she did have the proof.

"I'm pregnant, and my baby was conceived that night. I had blood work done at two weeks that can date my pregnancy to that day, and I can have an ultrasound done to back that up."

The lawyer was quiet for a moment and Lucy could hear the blood pounding in her ears.

"Interesting. My client didn't mention any of this to me so honestly I'm not sure what to make of it. Did you tell my client about your pregnancy?"

"I told him a few days ago. I don't know why he didn't tell you yet. Maybe he was trying to protect me."

"Possibly, Miss Neel, and not without reason. I'll be completely honest with you—the pregnancy might provide a nice alibi, on the face of it. But in light of your very casual acquaintance with Mr. West at the time, it's likely that the prosecutor will assert that you could have slept with any number of men while staying at the ranch in Texas. And frankly if you did you'd be wise to tell me now."

Lucy felt a surge of anger rising within her and she struggled to control it. She wasn't going to be able to help Bowie if she flew off the handle and alienated his lawyer.

"I didn't sleep with anyone else. Bowie, Mr. West, was the first and only man I've ever slept with in my life."

"You are over legal age, I take it."

"I'm twenty-seven years old, Mr. Crane."

By the time she hung up the phone Lucy was shaking. Her rage was white-hot. She wanted to punch or kick something, preferably Bowie's lawyer.

She could see that coming forward and standing up for Bowie in a court of law was going to take every ounce of strength and self-control she was capable of mustering.

The humiliation of the conversation she'd just had would pale in comparison to what the prosecutor would try to do to her.

For a moment she wasn't sure she could do it. Could she see her name in the papers labeled as a cheap date, an easy score, a loose woman? Could she come forward and show herself as a woman had made the age-old mistake of getting "knocked up" by a man she barely knew?

She cringed inwardly at the prospect of seeing herself cast in that negative light.

But if she didn't do it, then Bowie might well

spend a decade or more behind bars. And she would be raising their child, alone, wondering "what if?"

Mr. Crane had said that he needed to discuss her proposal with his client, and Lucy knew that she needed to do the same. She didn't want Bowie to turn down her offer to testify, so she decided to drive to the Travis County jail during visiting hours, to convince him. Apparently, you could video chat with prisoners from your own computer at home, but that took a day to get approved and she didn't want to waste time.

As Lucy pocketed her parking stub and walked nervously toward the correctional building, she couldn't help thinking what a strange and brutal string of circumstances her little fling had gotten her into.

"I'm here to see Bowie West."

"Is he expecting you?"

"No."

She gave her name and was told to go and sit in a hard plastic chair in front of a screen. Apparently there were no face-to-face meetings anymore. There were other people nearby, talking in hushed tones to other screens. She tried not to listen to their conversations as she knew she wouldn't want them to listen to hers.

She sat there for at least fifteen minutes and was ready to give up, when she saw Bowie walk into the room being recorded by the monitor.

The guard indicated where he should sit, and he moved slowly toward the chair. His bearing was tense, his features set with anger, and when he finally looked up at her she saw something in his eyes that made her planned greeting catch in her throat.

She fumbled with the telephone-like microphone,

and Bowie, his mouth an unmoving line, followed her actions and picked up the phone on his side.

"Hi, Bowie." The words were barely audible.

"I didn't want you to come here," Bowie said quietly.

"I know. I had to, though. I told your lawyer that I can provide an alibi for the night of September fourth."

"He told me." Bowie looked at her, still unsmiling, his eyes searching her face.

"I want to help you, Bowie."

"You'll regret it. They'll tear you apart on the stand."

"I know. I'm tough, I can take it. I don't care what people say about me."

"You don't deserve this, Lucy. I wish I'd never got you mixed up in this."

"It was all my doing. I seduced you, remember?" She tried to sound breezy. Which wasn't easy under the circumstances. "Are you okay in here?"

"I'm all right. Don't worry about me. How are you and the baby doing?"

Lucy didn't want to mention that doing the work alone tired her. Bowie had enough to worry about already. "We're doing fine. You have to tell the courts that you have an alibi for that night."

Bowie blew out hard. "I don't want you to have to stand up in court and say, 'He couldn't have done it your honor because we were making the beast with two backs at the time.' That's just not right. Especially now that I know..." Bowie looked down.

"That I was a virgin."

Bowie looked up at her, and his sad expression caused a knot to form in her gut. "I doubt anyone will believe that in court of a woman as beautiful as you."

She was trying so hard to be cool, calm and hardboiled, but the tenderness in his eyes almost broke her resolve.

She wanted more than anything to reach though the video monitor, to hold him, to tell him it was going to be okay. She wished she could believe it was.

"I didn't like your lawyer much. Is he good?"

"He's the best. He didn't say anything to you, anything offensive, did he? If he did, I'll..." She could see anger stiffening Bowie's back.

"No, no, he was testing me, I think, to see how I'd hold up on the stand. If he's good, then I'll do whatever he thinks is right."

"You don't have to do this, Lucy."

"I know, but I want to." She'd tried to keep her emotions on a short leash, but they'd already gotten away from her. She did care about Bowie. Not just because they were going to have a baby together, but because he was kind, thoughtful, fun, sweet, a great cook, amazing in bed.... There was no end to the reasons she found herself falling for him.

Of course, he was also a wealthy, famous, and successful rodeo star with a ranch was so vast he didn't know where it ended. These things sounded like positives but where actually negatives if you were just an ordinary girl who hoped to enjoy a quite private life with the person.

Bowie's lawyer managed to get a hearing scheduled. The idea was to examine evidence and see if there was enough to go to trial, or if charges should be dropped. It was less than a month away. Lucy wondered at the wisdom of this, since it didn't give them much time to find the real culprit, but apparently Bowie's lawyer was under strict orders from his client to get things moving at the earliest possible date because he still hoped to ride in the big bull riding championship in October.

Once she got approved, she was able to video chat with him. He talked a lot about the upcoming rodeos on the schedule. She could tell he was trying to see his current situation as a temporary setback and looking ahead to resuming his life. He'd missed one important rodeo, but he already had enough points to qualify for the finals. The prospect of going still made his eyes light up, so she hoped and prayed he'd really be able to.

Bowie always asked how she was feeling and insisted that she not do too much hard work while she was pregnant. His brother Jesse sent over an enthusiastic kid named Stevie from his own ranch to help with the daily chores and any handyman projects. Bowie had arranged to have Stevie's wages paid weekly, despite Lucy's vigorous protests, and would not be moved.

When she sat at her computer, she and Bowie talked excitedly about the things they would do together once he was free. Lucy was glad to see that his time under lock and key had not yet extinguished the sparkle of enthusiasm in his eyes, and she suspected that their daily talks were partly responsible.

There were moments though, when she could see that the prospect of ten, twenty, or even thirty years in prison was ever present in Bowie's mind, haunting him even as he tried to enjoy his few precious minutes with her. He told her his lawyer had insisted he not discuss the case as his video chats with her could be recorded and entered as evidence, so she couldn't even ask him if his lawyers had found the real killer or any new evidence. Nothing in the news suggested that any progress had been made, and as far as she knew, Bowie's hopes for freedom rested with her testimony.

Whatever it takes, she told herself, *if I can do it, I will.*

15

Lucy was extremely nervous on the day of the hearing. She wore a conservative navy suit that Val had helped her pick out and tied a dark silk scarf at her neck. With her curls wrangled into a neat bun, she looked like the furthest thing anyone could imagine from a "loose woman." Her nerves jangling, she giggled at the thought that seeing her in this frumpy getup might put Bowie right off her. *Deep breaths. Focus, relax, and don't let the prosecutor get you rattled.*

The hearing was in the afternoon and she attempted to eat a sandwich for lunch but her stomach was too jumpy. Jesse met her outside the courtroom and introduced her to his and Bowie's brother Daniel. Daniel was the tallest yet, with black hair and cool gray eyes. He barely spoke beyond a brief greeting, then looked around the courtroom as if he were studying animals at the zoo.

The usually calm and unflappable Jesse seemed agitated. "Bowie's lawyer wanted to postpone but Bowie wouldn't let him. He says's he's got some new evidence and wanted more time to build a case. He think's Bowie is too confident that the judge will see the truth and find him innocent."

"He knows I'll stand up as his alibi."

"I just hope they'll believe you."

Jesse pointed out Bowie's father, a distinguished looking older man, and his brother Shane. Both dressed in well-cut gray suits, they looked more like corporate executives than ranchers. They sat on the opposite side of the courtroom, far away from the lawyers and the rest of the family. Tall and handsome like his brothers, Shane had a cold, distant look to him. It was impossible to imagine him riding a horse, let alone a bull.

Did they know she was pregnant with Bowie's baby—which would be his father's first grandson? She suspected not, since she knew Bowie was somewhat estranged from his father. She wondered grimly how they'd react when they found out—which they most certainly would when she testified.

Bowie wore a gray suit like his father, but even in the dull uniform of conformity he had a rakish, piratical look to him. She hoped the judge wouldn't hold it against him.

The prosecutor laid out the "facts," which pointed very damningly at Bowie, what with the victim's deodorant stick found in his bathroom and his finger prints on the murder weapon. He also showed horrible crime scene photos, then sat down with a flourish as if the conviction was a done deal.

Lucy's heart beat so fast she could barely breathe. She wanted to get up and yell that Bowie was innocent. She could see that Jesse was similarly agitated. He kept shifting in his seat and forming a fist, then wrapping it with his other hand. Daniel sat there as if he were made of stone. Every now and then she snuck a glance at Bowie's father and Shane, and neither of them betrayed a hint of emotion.

Bowie's lawyer, Bill Crane, launched into an aggressive rebuttal of the "evidence," saying—as she had suspected—that each of the items had been planted, and that the murder weapon must have been stolen from Bowie's collection. Her heart sank when she realized how unconvincing that probably sounded to the judge. And what kind of innocent person had a big gun collection?

There was one surprise though, and it made Bowie's father sit up in astonishment. Crane said that they'd found a connection between Terri Balboa and the West family. She had been seen on several occasions with a man named Russell Jenkins, who was the foreman of the main West ranch, where the older West and Shane lived, and a friend of the victim's had confirmed that they had a relationship.

This was apparently news to the prosecutor, who had a hurried whispered conversation with the man next to him, who then rushed out of the room. Jesse and Daniel seemed stunned, too, and kept looking over to where their father was sitting.

Crane then said he had a key witness to call— her—who would provide a confirmed alibi for Bowie at the time of the murder. The judge called for a break and voices buzzed and hummed around her like a swarm of angry bees.

Lucy had a horrible thought. Why was the ranch foreman involved? Was Bowie's father somehow behind this? Did he want to get his rebellious, hard-to-control son out of the picture for some reason—possibly to get his hands on the land Bowie wouldn't sell back to him.

She kept her thoughts to herself.

After the break Lucy was led to the stand and forced to swear to tell the truth, the whole truth, and nothing but the truth.

Her pulse pounded in her skull, and her hands shook with nerves as she ascended to the witness box. Bill Crane, Bowie's lawyer, questioned her first, and she knew his goal was to help her present her information in a compelling and convincing way. He asked a lot of questions that required little more than a "yes" or "no" answer:

"Were you with Bowie West all night on the night of September fourth?" and "Did Mr. West have an opportunity to leave the room at any time between 10 p.m. and 5 a.m.?" Lucy was grateful that he made the process as painless as possible.

The judge was given a file of paperwork from her doctor, the blood test that dated her pregnancy and a subsequent ultrasound, with pictures, that corroborated the exact date of conception.

Lucy found her hand straying to her belly as she listened to Bowie's lawyer. "As you can see, your honor, the results of these blood tests prove that conception could only have occurred during the time in question, and thus the whereabouts of my client at that time can be proved beyond a reasonable doubt."

As Crane walked back to his seat, Lucy shot a glance at Bowie. He watched her intently, his hands clasped tightly in front of him, his jaw set. He caught her eyes for a brief second and a muscle twitched in his cheek. She could see that he was afraid for her.

His concern touched her, when his own predicament was so much worse. Bowie's future literally depended on her.

She and Bowie had known each other for such a short time, and in that time she'd grown into a new person. She'd started out as a lonely woman who'd never had a real relationship and just wanted to seize a night of romance so she'd know what all the fuss was about and wouldn't feel so left out.

To her surprise she'd met a strong, kind, charming and exciting man who she'd fallen head over heels in love with.

Maybe she'd even found the possibility of a lifetime of companionship and joy. Something she hadn't even dared to hope for before she met Bowie.

She wasn't going to let the prosecutor take that away from her. Not if she could help it.

Lucy heard a menacing hush fall over the courtroom as the prosecutor approached the stand. She took a deep breath.

"Miss Neel. The prosecution does not dispute the fact that you are pregnant, and that your baby was conceived on September fourth of this year. In the absence of DNA testing, however, there is no way to determine if the baby is the issue of Mr. Bowie West, or of one of the many other men who were no doubt in residence with you at the Singing Pines Ranch on the date in question."

Lucy looked at him silently, biting her tongue.

"You do assert, I take it, that the baby is Mr. West's?"

"Of course."

"A yes or no answer will suffice."

"Yes."

"Would you agree to undergo the procedure known as amniocentesis in order to extract DNA from the uterus and prove that the baby is Mr.

West's?"

"Objection!" Mr. Crane rose from his chair. "Amniocentesis cannot be done before fourteen weeks, your honor."

"I repeat the question, would you be willing to do the test once you reach fourteen weeks."

"Yes," Lucy said. Her voice was barely above a whisper. She'd have to wait another six weeks before even doing the test. That would be an eternity behind bars for poor Bowie, and he'd miss the finals. Still, it was better than the alternative.

"Did I hear you agree?"

"Yes. I'll do it."

Lucy had not been planning to have the procedure, which was used mainly to establish the presence or absence of genetic abnormalities. She was too young for a likelihood of genetic abnormalities, and the risk of amniocentesis was a 1 in 200 chance of losing the baby to a miscarriage.

Against her better judgment she glanced over at Bowie, who looked as if he was about to rise out of his chair. His face was blazing with emotion that he was struggling to keep in under control.

"Your honor, may I approach the bench." Mr. Crane had risen again. The judge gave him permission and a whispered conversation ensued at the bench between the Judge, Mr. Crane and the Prosecutor.

When they returned to their seats, the prosecutor approached Lucy.

"There is another possibility, however, a procedure known as Chorionic Villus Sampling, or CVS. It is similar to amniocentesis but in this case the genetic material is extracted from the placenta rather than the amniotic fluid. This procedure can be done as early as eight weeks, so we would be able to schedule you for an appointment immediately.

"I must caution you, however, that the risks of this procedure are rather higher than those of Amniocentesis. CVS carries a 1 in 100 risk of miscarriage."

Lucy swallowed hard. 1 in 100. But she had to do it. From where she was sitting, Bowie had about a 1 in 1 chance of being convicted and spending the best years of his life in prison. The baby's odds were still better than that.

"I'll do it."

"No! Don't do it Lucy!" Bowie was on his feet and a bailiff stood up to restrain him. Lucy prayed that he wasn't going to do anything to compound his legal troubles.

The judged banged his gavel loudly on his desk, "Order! Order! Order in court. A ten minute recess ladies and gentlemen."

Lucy sat anxiously on the uncomfortable bench, conscious of people looking at her and whispering about her behind their hands.

Twice she caught Bowie's eye as he sat stoically in his hard wooden chair. She could see he was using all the restraint he possessed to try to keep his thoughts and emotions in check in this room full of hostile strangers.

Lucy longed to reach out to him through the din of the courtroom, to run a hand through his hair, to stroke his cheek, to kiss his eyelids, to rest her head on his shoulder and tell him it was all going to be all right.

If things didn't go their way she might never have

the chance to do those things again. If Bowie lost his case, their only future contact would be hushed conversations through a scratched sheet of plexiglass—or worse, via video.

Bowie, I need you so much. And our baby needs you.

When the judge came in, he looked grave. He shuffled his papers, still standing, then cleared his throat.

"This is an unusual measure, but one that I feel is justified in this most unusual situation. Miss Lucinda Neel agreed unhesitatingly to immediate Chorionic Villus Sampling to determine the paternity of her baby, a risk that she would not have taken lightly, and certainly not if the procedure was likely to prove her a liar.

"As judge of this court I am now firmly convinced that Bowie West is indeed the responsible party in this pregnancy. I can see no further need to endanger the health of Ms. Neel or her fetus by pursuing unnecessary invasive surgery.

"Furthermore, since Miss Neel's testimony provides Mr. West with a cast iron alibi for the night in question, the guilt of Mr. West in the murder of Terri Balboa on the night of September fourth is certainly open to reasonable doubt. In light of the new evidence that a West family insider—someone who might have had access to Bowie West's personal effects—was in fact acquainted with the victim, I am not convinced that there is enough evidence to pursue a trial at the present time. Mr. West will be immediately released from jail."

The judge immediately left the courtroom, which exploded into a roar of chatter.

Lucy swallowed. That was good, right? Of course

it would be better if he was declared innocent, but at least he'd be able to resume his rodeo career.

She sprang to her feet, her eyes fixed on Bowie, who let big grin creep across his face. The bailiffs conferred for a moment before simply opening up the dock and telling him he was free to leave.

Bowie picked his way impatiently across the courtroom, finally vaulting over two rows of benches that barred his way, and hurled himself toward Lucy. He hugged her so tightly she thought she might burst.

"You did it! You set me free. Oh, Lucy, it feels so good to hold you again." Lucy didn't know what to say—he wasn't really free, not for good—so she just held him back.

She wondered if he would introduce her to his father and his brother Shane, but when she turned to look for them they'd already left the courtroom. Daniel and Jesse hugged him and insisted they all go out for a drink before they headed back to their respective homes.

"I don't know how to thank you, Lucy," said Jesse, who hadn't stopped grinning since the judge's announcement. "You've given our brother back to us."

"You can thank me by being caring uncles to our child." It was a bold thing to say. She couldn't guarantee that she and Bowie would even last. But she already felt a bond with these big strong men who seemed they could carry the world on their broad shoulders.

"I'll teach the kid how to ride," said Jesse. "I mean really ride, not just stay on for eight seconds." Bowie mock punched him. "And Daniel will teach him how to talk to animals."

"Please feel free to count on me for whatever you need," said the far more serious Daniel.

"I appreciate it," she said with a smile. Already these three big men felt like family, and they'd all survived an ordeal that had brought them closer.

After they ate, Bowie said that he wanted to go back to Lucy's ranch. They climbed into her pickup and sped away from the city, emotional and sexual tension crackling between them like rogue electrical currents in the tight space of the truck's cab.

"It sounds presumptuous of me to call it home, but that's how I've been thinking of your ranch lately. There were times in the last month where I was sorely tested, but I just focused on getting back to you and our baby in one piece, as soon as possible."

His tie was loosened and he looked like he was able to breathe freely for the first time that day. The windows were open and the cool evening air tossed his hair in a way that made Lucy smile. She had Bowie back, whole, unscathed, and all hers.

All hers. Was it really possible?

16

"You cannot imagine how relieved I was when the judge said you were free to go."

"Believe me, I can." Bowie turned to look at her and they both laughed.

When they arrived back at the ranch, Bowie didn't want to go straight into the house. He wanted to walk around outside and see the trees, the stars, the horses, illuminated by the nearly full moon.

"High Pastures Ranch has really got a hold on me, much like the lovely lady who owns it." He slipped his arms around her waist and planted a warm kiss on her lips. "I've been to a lot of places in my life, but I've never wanted to go back to any of them as much as I've longed to come back here. I felt lost without you, Lucy."

Bowie cupped Lucy's face in his hands. He kissed her eyelids, her forehead, her cheeks, her chin, then finally her mouth, which opened to his, their tongues winding around each other as their arms reached for each other.

They kissed and held each other, then Bowie lifted his head and looked at Lucy.

"You made a huge sacrifice coming forward to stand up for me. I'd never have asked you to do that.

You risked being publicly ridiculed."

"I don't care what people say about me. I just wanted you to be free. I wanted you back."

"If they'd made you have that procedure, and something had happened to our baby—" Bowie looked aside and exhaled sharply.

"They didn't leave me any choice. I couldn't take the chance of letting them lock you away." She paused, unsure if she should say the words that rose to her lips. *I love you.*

She kept them to herself. She didn't want to put more pressure on him when he was under so much already.

Bowie looked at her silently for a moment. His eyes were unreadable in the darkness of the night.

The physical attraction between them had grown and changed into something far more substantial, and they could both feel it.

I need you, Bowie. I need you. She reached up and pulled his face to hers, drinking in the scent of his skin. How she'd missed that warm smell that was all Bowie. She settled her mouth his and felt his arms tighten around her as their emotional connection heated into a powerful physical need to touch each other, to hold each other, to bury themselves in each other.

Bowie's hands roved up and down her back, pulling up the jacket of her suit and the blouse she was wearing, anxious to feel her warm skin. He sighed with honest relief and she felt herself relaxing for the first time in weeks, letting herself go, allowing herself to fall into Bowie's arms and feel safe.

Their kisses grew longer and deeper, their mouths covering each other, tasting and sucking, drinking in each other's hunger and longing.

At last Bowie drew back from her an inch or two, and Lucy opened her eyes. His green eyes roved over her face, so close to his, and his features had that odd expression of amazement that she couldn't seem to get used to.

"Why do you always look so astonished when we kiss?"

"Because I am astonished, floored, flummoxed, bowled over…" He shook his head, smiling. "When we kiss, something about you takes hold of me and lifts me out of myself. It's the craziest sensation, it makes bull riding feel like sitting on a log by comparison."

Lucy could feel the heat of his desire rising from his body. He still wore the suit from his courtroom appearance. "I know you think you look good in a suit, but I'm not so sure."

"You think I'd look better out of a suit?" asked Bowie, raising an eyebrow ever so slightly.

"Shall we go inside?" asked Lucy with a half smile.

"Lead the way, lady," said Bowie, with a tip of a pretend hat. He slapped her behind. "I'll race you." Then he took off for the house, laughing. "Come on!"

They ran together, fumbled with the lock to open the door, and once inside Bowie grabbed her hand and pulled her up the stairs.

They burst into the bedroom and hit the bed together. Lucy pushed off Bowie's suit jacket while he teased her, nibbling along her jawline and sticking his tongue in her ear.

She unbelted his pants and struggled to push them down while his tongue tormented her, hot on the pulse point behind her ear. She tried to unbutton his shirt but the fiddly little buttons were too much for her. She abandoned it to put her hands in Bowie's hair, pulling his face over hers, hungrily biting and sucking each beloved feature that she'd dreamed about over the past lonely weeks.

She moaned with longing, and Bowie seemed to sense the urgency of her need. Not taking the time to remove her clothes, he pushed up the skirt and put a warm hand over her hot sex.

She was ready. He moved over her—still kissing and tasting her face with his hot mouth—and sank in. Lucy let out a cry of pleasure and relief to feel Bowie inside her.

She hugged him to her as he moved inside her. He was gasping and murmuring in her ear, and she could feel every muscle of his body alive with sensation and focused only on moving with her, filling her, holding her, traveling with her on this journey of intimacy and passion.

She'd been willing to give up her reputation for him with no more care than if it was yesterday's crumpled newspaper. What people thought about her was meaningless compared to the joy of being able to hold Bowie in her arms again. She wanted to hold him in her arms for the rest of her life.

Their long month of waiting had built their need for each other to a fevered intensity that made both of them move in gyrating rhythms of frenzied desperation. Lucy's blood sang in her ears and strange images danced before her eyes. Disconcerted, she opened them and saw Bowie's face contorted with pleasure, with the intensity of the moment, his eyes tightly shut.

His eyes opened, wide and startlingly green and at that instant he gasped and she could feel Bowie losing control of himself, spilling over the edge and into her. She felt her own body rushing to join him, and she abandoned all control and flowed with him, blood and muscle pulsing and throbbing as a sob of relief caught in her throat.

They lay collapsed together on the bed. The crumpled ruins of their courtroom clothes were damp with perspiration.

Sitting up, he carefully unbuttoned her suit jacket and blouse, and slipped off her skirt. Then he pulled the comforter up over her, removed his own remaining clothes and climbed under the covers with her. Happiness welled in her chest. It was so good to have him back in her bed. She'd lived alone her whole adult life, but since she met Bowie her house didn't feel like a home without him in it.

"I missed your crazy cooking."

Bowie chuckled. "I'll have your eyes burning with curry powder again before too long, don't you worry."

They held each other close and drifted to sleep with their limbs intertwined, hoping that life, and the prosecutors office, would never force them to sleep any other way again.

"You can ride in the big rodeo now."

"Sure can." He kissed her nose. "Vegas, here I come."

"That's great." She tried to keep a hint of sadness out of her voice. She didn't want to lose him again so soon. "And you're allowed to travel wherever you want now?"

"Yep. My lawyer hopes they'll drop the case. The

police brought my dad's foreman in for questioning while we were driving back today. If he confesses, I'm home free. Just thinking about it makes me want to yell from the rooftops."

"That might scare the horses." She pressed her smile against his cheek.

"Yeah. So I'll just make love to you again, instead."

It wasn't easy being pregnant with the baby of a famous bull rider. Especially when it happened by accident—on your first time.

Lucy glanced sideways at the gorgeous man who'd turned her life upside down. He'd only been at her ranch a few days and already every one of her female boarders, from grandmas to giggling teenagers, was heated and unsettled by the presence of the "new ranch hand," as he called himself.

If his flashing green eyes, sun-streaked hair and mischievous charm weren't distracting enough, he had a disturbing tendency to remove his shirt while he was working, revealing an expanse of tanned, muscled chest and a strong back ornamented by a tattooed tiger with as much feline grace as its owner.

He wasn't hers, though. Not in any kind of permanent way. He didn't kiss her in front of people, or put his arm around her or playfully squeeze her butt.

He only did those things when they were alone together. In the privacy of her house she got to live out the fantasy that Bowie West was hers—only hers—but outside that cocoon he gave her no illusions.

Maybe it was her fault. She didn't want everyone

to think they were an item and then to feel sorry for her when he vanished, so she kept him at arms length. If anyone knew she was pregnant, they kept it to themselves. And they might well know—she'd spoken about her pregnancy in court get Bowie off the hook for a murder charge. She was his alibi for the night of the shooting. It was hard to imagine the story didn't get covered somewhere, but maybe his influential family had hushed it up. Or maybe people were just being polite and recognizing that it was none of their business.

But the world outside was calling him. The big bull riding finals in Vegas were only two days away.

"What are you going to do without me, huh?" He snuck up behind her in her kitchen, breath all hot on her neck. "Will you miss me?"

"I'll be fine." She was trying to convince herself as much as him. She didn't want him to know how much she'd come to count on him in her life. How much her heart ached at the prospect of losing him.

"You should come watch." He stroked her cheek with his thumb.

"Come to Vegas? You know I can't do that. I have a business to run." She tried to sound serious, which was hard with his hands suddenly roaming up the front of her body. "I have twenty-three horses to take care of and lessons to teach."

"You have Stevie to help you." Bowie was still paying for him to come every day. "He could take over while you're gone."

"Do you really think running a barn is so easy that some kid with strong muscles can do it?" Maybe he didn't take her work seriously. It was probably pretty easy to blow off her small business when he'd inherited a fortune. "Keeping my clients happy is a big part of my business. There's plenty of competition around. I can't just take off whenever I feel like it."

"Sure you can." He laid a soft kiss on her lips that made her belly quiver and almost melted her resolve.

"I can't. I've boarded at barns where the owner did that, and as soon as she's out of earshot everyone starts gossiping and backbiting and before you know it they're all moving to a barn down the road."

"Which might not be such a bad thing. You're pregnant. You should take it easy."

"What?" Now she was mad. She put her hand flat on his chest and pushed him back a little. "You have no idea how hard I've worked to build this place. It may not seem like much to you but it's everything to me. How would you feel if I told you that you should quit your rodeo career because it's too dangerous now that you're going to be a father."

She regretted the words the moment they passed her lips.

His body stiffened and she watched surprise crystalize in his eyes. "You think I should quit bull riding?"

"No, of course not." The words rushed out. "I'm trying to prove a point. That me asking you to give up bull riding is as ridiculous as you asking me to give up running my barn."

"Oh." His gaze softened. How would he feel if she did start to make those kinds of demands on him? Or any demands. Their relationship had started as a one-night stand and neither of them knew where it would end. "Are you worried that I'll get hurt?"

"No."

Yes. Of course she was. She hadn't fallen off a

horse in…years. She couldn't even remember the last time. With rodeo riding you got on the horse or bull pretty much knowing you were going to fall off each and every time. The only question was how long you could hang in there before it happened.

"You don't care about me?" A lifted brow accompanied the question. But the ever present humor in his eyes told her not to take it too seriously.

"You're an experienced professional. You'll do your best not to get hurt." She tried to sound cool and impersonal. "Just like you know I plan to ride while I'm pregnant and be very careful about it."

He nodded. "We're alike in a lot of ways."

"Are we?" She couldn't really see it. He was tall, famous, athletic, and mega wealthy. She was shortish, plumpish, unknown outside her circle of friends, and she knew how to squeeze a dollar until it screamed.

"We both ride horses." He leaned into her again, his hard chest brushing against her nipples.

Heat flashed through her. "You ride bulls," she teased.

"And horses."

"Okay, you're a pretty decent rider, I have to admit, even if you do ride western."

"You could give me some English riding lessons."

"Only if you'll wear the full outfit, including breeches and a velvet hat."

He was now so close that his spicy male scent filled her senses and made it hard to breathe. "Nobody wears those velvet hats any more. They're all made of titanium or something."

"True." She giggled. His chest crushed her breasts gently but firmly, stirring a mess of sensations inside her. "But the tall black leather boots are a must."

She didn't find out how he felt about the boots because his mouth closed over hers, hot and urgent, kissing her thoughts into oblivion.

A sigh escaped her as his strong arms closed around her, gathering her tightly against his chest. Being in Bowie's arms felt so right, like they were meant to be together and nothing could separate them.

Her fingers surprised her by wandering to the waistband of his jeans and sliding inside. The feel of his hard backside sent lust rushing through her. She'd never known serious arousal like this before she met Bowie. Maybe that's why she'd been able to cruise through her life alone, with only a long-distance "boyfriend" on the back burner.

He sucked her neck gently, and the intense sensation made her arch against him and grip his butt tighter. She could feel his hard arousal pressing against the zipper of his jeans and it made heat rush through her. Next thing she knew she was struggling with his zipper and shoving his jeans down over his hips.

"Uh oh, I think we're going to do it right here in your kitchen."

17

Bowie lifted Lucy's T-shirt and buried his face between her breasts, which made her giggle. Her whole body was so hot right now she felt it could burst into flames at any moment.

He unzipped her breeches and pushed them down over her ankles, then lifted her up onto her kitchen counter. The cool granite under her rear end made her squeal but only heightened the intense rush of sensations flooding her body.

He was already shirtless, and she ran her hands over the rippling muscles of his broad back and sturdy arms. She'd seen how strong he was as he lifted bales of hay and hammered nails into fencing around her farm. His body was ripped from hard work—and hard play in the rodeo ring—not from lifting weights in a gym, and that made him even sexier.

He eased her into position over his erection, then slid into her slowly, kissing her hard enough to take her breath away while he did it. Emotion rushed through her as he filled her, and she clung to him, gasping at the feelings that stormed her body and mind.

I do love him.

She half wished she didn't. She had no business loving a man as successful and desirable as Bowie West. He belonged to the world, not to her.

And she didn't dare tell him. That might scare him off. She was carrying his baby, and he was hers for now, and that would have to be enough.

Bowie's big hands wrapped around her backside and eased her against him as he rocked them both, alternating between nuzzling her breasts through her bra and kissing her intently on the mouth.

She felt her orgasm building inside her and she tried to hold it back, but the rippling, rising contractions overwhelmed her and she felt her insides grip and squeeze him as her stomach fluttered against his chest. Her own moans of ecstasy filled the kitchen and bounced off the fridge and the walls, soon joined by Bowie's guttural agreements.

"Unbelievable," he murmured, burying his face in her neck. "You slay me."

She smiled. She could tell he was aroused by her, which surprised and amazed her but also thrilled her. Who knew a man like Bowie would enjoy a woman with full, rounded curves?

But he hadn't said he loved her. It was too soon for that anyway. She was jumping the gun with her own feelings and she knew she should hold back. Their relationship was on fast-forward only because she'd accidentally gotten pregnant on their first crazy date. If she hadn't, they probably would have gone their separate ways and she'd have never seen him again.

She'd never have known that he owned half the town she lived in. He hadn't even known it himself. That's how damn rich he was.

Her heart sank again. There was no future between her and Bowie, so she might as well make the most of this. "How do you do this to me?"

"Get you bare-assed on your own kitchen counter?" Those green eyes glittered with amusement.

"Exactly!" She wasn't the spontaneous type. She had a strict routine—like anyone with horses—and rarely veered from it.

"What can I say? You're too much for me. I couldn't help myself." He stroked her lips with his thumb. "You're a very sexy lady."

She giggled. "I wonder if the doctor would approve of me doing this while I'm pregnant."

"There's nothing wrong with having sex while you're pregnant. I checked." His expression was serious.

"What? With who?"

"On the Internet. I don't want to do anything to harm our baby."

"Warmth filled her heart. "That's sweet of you to be concerned enough to check. Did it say anything about sex on countertops?"

"Not that I saw. I did read that you shouldn't be doing a lot of heavy lifting or very strenuous exercise, so you must make sure that Stevie does all the hard work while I'm away."

"Okay. I promise I'll be good." She wiggled on the countertop. She wanted to laugh that she was promising to be "good" while sitting her naked amongst the pots and pans for the dinner they hadn't even made yet.

Would he be "good" while he was in Vegas? She didn't dare ask. He certainly had a reputation with the ladies and there were bound to be girls all around him. He was already one of the top three contenders for the world title and that alone would get the ladies excited—add in his gorgeous looks and his wealth and…

She sighed.

"What's the matter?"

"Nothing." She didn't want to seem clingy or a nuisance. And although she wished he weren't going to Vegas, she knew she should keep that to herself. He'd invited her, after all. He wouldn't do that if he was planning to sleep with other women. "I'm fine. This is all a little overwhelming."

"I understand." He helped her carefully off the counter and back into her panties and jeans. "Just being pregnant must be hard to wrap your mind around. I still can't believe I'm going to be a father."

"You'll be a fantastic father." *Even if we're not together.* She didn't want to get her hopes up, but she did want him in their child's life.

She turned on the oven—right next to the counter where they'd just had sex—and pulled some chicken breasts out of the fridge to season.

"I hope I'll be better than mine, at least."

"He was cold?" She'd seen him at the hearing. He barely glanced at his son.

"Never had any time for me. He was only interested in having an heir who could run the business. That's my brother Shane. The rest of us barely exist to him. My mom raised us and luckily she was his total opposite—warm and kind and loving."

"And she left you the ranch next to mine." She salted and peppered the chicken, then added her own hot-pepper blend.

"Yes. My dad loved her so much he had her listed

as a co-owner of all his property. I guess she was worried about us getting shut out of his will, so she left us all big tracts of it when she died. She must have known he wouldn't want to disrespect her memory by fighting the will, so he keeps trying to buy them back. I think it galls him that his own sons own and control land he's always considered his."

"Doesn't he own tens of thousands of acres already? What would he do with five thousand more?"

"Exploit it for oil, most likely. Drilling technology has changed a lot in the last few decades so they can extract oil from land previously considered useless or exhausted. It ruins the land, though, and pollutes the water for miles around."

"Fracking?"

"Exactly. There's more of it happening in the Hill Country all the time."

Lucy shuddered. Bowie's ranch wrapped right around hers. "That would be a nightmare."

"Don't worry. I'm not going to sell."

But a dark thought occurred to her. "Is your father the type of person who might try to frame you for murder just to get his hands on the land?"

Bowie frowned. "I don't think my dad would frame me for murder. He doesn't exactly have fond feelings for me but he wouldn't do anything to tarnish the family name. He hates publicity with a passion. He didn't manage to cover up the initial story of the murder. That was everywhere, which means he wasn't in control of the situation."

"I know. That's how I learned about it. But if it wasn't him, then someone else framed you, and you need to figure out who." She didn't like the idea that a person out there meant harm—a life sentence or worse, since Texas had the death penalty—for Bowie.

"Right now the only things I'm concerned about are winning my next rodeo and making passionate love to my sexy woman." He wrapped his arms around her with so much force that she dropped the potato peeler. He spun her around and kissed her, heating her blood and making her forget about everything but how good it felt to be right here, right now, in Bowie's arms.

Lucy put on a brave face the day Bowie left for Vegas. She wished him luck and told him to be careful—then regretted the last part. It made her sound clingy and she'd resolved not to cramp his style.

She'd also resolved to stay away from all press coverage of the big rodeo, which went on for days. She didn't want to see Bowie surrounded by adoring fans, and she didn't fancy seeing him get tossed around by a bull, either.

But her best friend Val wouldn't leave her alone. She showed up at Lucy's ranch at lunchtime with a delicious picnic of French bread and cold cuts. "I'm going to make sure you eat properly and don't overdo it while Bowie is gone." She set out the picnic on the outdoor table that looked over the paddocks.

"You're crazy. Since when have I ever had trouble eating properly? And Stevie is here to help. He won't let me do anything. It's driving me nuts."

"Good." Val grinned. "Check out this video of Bowie's ride last night." She pulled out her phone and started scrolling.

"No! I don't want to see it. It will raise my blood

pressure."

"Have you ever seen him ride, like, at all?"

Lucy bit her lip. "I saw him do a demo ride at Singing Pines."

"Watch this. Believe me, you'll enjoy it."

Lucy sighed and took the phone from Val. The tiny video showed Bowie in the chute, waiting for his ride to start. She gasped as he exploded out into the ring on the back of a big black bull. The bull span and leapt like a bucking bronco. "I can't watch this!" But she couldn't drag her eyes away. Bowie stayed glued to the bull's back like he was rolling on top of ocean waves. When the bell rang he jumped free as if he were hopping off a bus. "Wow."

"See? I told you that you'd like it."

She watched Bowie's athletic body as he ran for the fence and vaulted over. "He's so strong."

"And gorgeous! And all yours."

"He's not all mine. I'm not delusional enough to think he's going to stay with me."

"Why not?"

"Because he's...Bowie West. And I'm just a regular person."

"What makes you think the great Bowie West doesn't want to marry a nice down-to-earth girl and enjoy a restful life?"

"I just know it. He's said himself that he's a rolling stone. He lives to travel around following the rodeo circuit. Settling down is not his thing. The best I can hope for is him coming to visit his kid when he's in town."

Val frowned. Clearly she could see that Lucy had a point. "Then you need to fix that."

Lucy laughed. "You can't change people. You of

all people should know that."

"Are you referring to my two divorces?"

"Only in the fondest possible way. You told me yourself you married each of them thinking they had great potential."

Val laughed. "And they were both gorgeous. It's quite annoying how you know so much about me."

"Enough to take your relationship advice with a grain of salt. I like Bowie a lot, but I don't want to get my hopes up and get crushed. It's safer to be sensible."

"Which means you shouldn't be sleeping with him."

Lucy opened her mouth. Then shut it. "You're right. I shouldn't sleep with him again." Her heart sank. "There's no way a romantic relationship could last long term so I should focus on being friends."

"Now you're talking like a crazy lady. Are you kidding me? Bowie West is hotter than my five-alarm salsa. Even if you only get a few months with him, you should enjoy it for all it's worth."

Lucy wanted to laugh, but she shook her head. "Val, have you forgotten I'm carrying his baby? I can't just walk away with a sigh when he dumps me. I'll need to see him and share our child with him for the rest of my life."

"True. That part does slightly suck, especially when the guy doesn't even remember to show up half the time like Tommy's dad." Val poured them both some more sparkling lemonade. "But you've gotta make lemonade. For this one I used fresh organic lemons, seltzer, and fine brown sugar."

"It's yummy." The tart yet sweet drink tickled her tongue. "Which is lucky because you have me more confused than ever."

"Go to Vegas. Seize the moment. I've heard all your excuses, but watching the man you're crazy about win a huge rodeo title is going to be one of those once-in-a-lifetime experiences you tell your grandchildren about."

"Grandchildren? I'm not even in the second trimester yet." She laughed. "And maybe he won't win."

"Wouldn't you like to be there if he does?"

"Sure, but…"

"But nothing. You can fly there in two and a half hours. There are a lot of flights, too."

Possibilities flashed through Lucy's mind. Watching Bowie would be fun, even if he didn't win. And he might appreciate her coming to support him. That's the kind of thing that would mean a lot to her. "You know what? You're right. I'm going to go."

"Yay!" Val jumped up and clapped her hands. Then whipped out her phone. "Quick, let's buy your plane ticket before you chicken out."

And just like that, she was on her way to Vegas.

18

Misgivings hit her the moment the plane touched down at the airport. Flying from Texas to Vegas she thought she'd be leaving the cowboy hats behind, but as she picked up her bag, rented a car and drove nervously toward her hotel, she saw more cowboy hats and boots than she'd seen in the past five years.

Rhinestone cowboys, most of them, here for the big event and all the surrounding festivities. But these were people who'd know Bowie West on sight and probably worship him like a king.

She'd booked pretty much the last room in the whole Vegas area—Val found it after she'd given up—and she drove right down the glittering strip and almost out of town again before she found her hotel on a dreary side street.

"Don't tell him you're coming! Surprise him." Val's advice had appealed to her at the time. She could always change her mind and back out at the last minute, right?

But now she'd come all the way here it felt foolish.

"Hey, Bowie, I'm in town. Wanna hang out?" How did she tell him now? He was probably busy every minute meeting with old friends and making new ones.

She checked in and changed into jeans and a cute new shirt. Luckily, she still fit into regular clothes. There was no way anyone could tell she was pregnant. Cowboy boots and a silver-and-turquoise necklace were the final cowgirl touch.

It was two in the afternoon by the time she was ready, and the rodeo went on most of the day, so she knew where to find Bowie. Gritting her teeth and gathering all her courage, she set out for the Thomas and Mack Center.

By the time she finally negotiated the packed parking lot and elbowed her way into the crammed arena, her heart was pounding like a drum. The din of the crowd was deafening as they cheered on a team of cowboys doing something with calves in the area.

She hadn't realized this place would be so huge or so packed. She'd bought a seat and couldn't even guess how to get to it. Not to mention that she didn't know much about rodeo so without anyone to explain the events she'd probably have trouble grasping what each one was about.

She pulled out her phone with trembling fingers. She could text him, right? That wasn't intrusive.

On the other hand, who would hear the quiet ping of a text in this maelstrom?

Maybe she should call him. She pulled up his number and her finger hovered over the call button. What if he was busy? What if—right now—he was sitting on the back of the meanest bucking bull out there, getting ready to explode into the arena?

Unlikely. She didn't see any bulls in the holding pens. Maybe he didn't have an event and was out enjoying a quiet dinner with friends.

Or with a woman.

Lucy! Get a grip and call him. You're a grown woman and you're carrying his baby.

Somehow that last part made her more nervous than ever, but she pushed the number and waited.

"Hey, Lucy."

"Hey." He had no idea she was here. They'd spoken last night, and every night, but only to give a quick rundown of the day's events and wish each other a good night. She'd given no hints that she intended to stalk him to Vegas.

The crowd roared at something just as he spoke so she didn't hear what he said. "What was that? It's kind of loud here."

"Where are you?" His voice sounded smooth and sexy as ever, right in her ear.

"Uh, at the bull riding finals. I thought I'd run into you, but there are a few more cowboys here than I'd expected."

"You're here? Right now?"

"Yep." Her chest tightened. Was he happy or horrified?

"Do you mean it? Where are you?"

"I'm…" She glanced around. "I'm under a big sign saying Acme Feed. And there's a green balloon in the shape of a cactus, and—"

"I see you. Hold tight. I'm coming in."

He cut off before she could respond. She grew hot thinking of his eyes on her and scanned the arena, but couldn't make him out in the throng. She knew how cattle must feel during sorting, as people pushed passed her and she tried not to lose her balance and get trampled underfoot.

A pair of strong arms grabbed her from behind and wrapped around her waist, making the breath rush out of her lungs. "I found you."

Bowie's warm breath heated her neck, then he spun her around and kissed her full on the mouth.

Right here in front of everyone.

Stars danced behind Lucy's eyelids as the kiss dazzled her and made her knees grow weak. She hugged Bowie so tight, amazed by how much she'd missed him. "I wanted to surprise you," she breathed when they finally pulled apart.

"You did." He grinned, eyes sparkling. "What made you change your mind?"

"I wanted to see you ride. I wanted to root for you."

"Now that you're here I feel at least ten steps closer to winning."

"Are you riding today?"

"Four o'clock, and then I'm taking you back to my hotel."

Lucy felt a smile creep across her face. She'd wondered if it was silly to book her own room, but she didn't want to impose on Bowie. Or be too dependent on him if things went south. "Why, I'd never allow myself to be alone with a gentleman in his hotel room. Any number of things could happen."

"Like making passionate love to him and getting pregnant?" Bowie murmured in her ear.

"Exactly. I'd never do that." She laughed, feeling so relaxed it was hard to believe how worried she'd been about coming.

"Then I'll have to abduct you by force."

"Promises, promises."

The were standing in a wide aisle with people rushing around them on all sides, and she didn't notice the photographer until the flash went off right in her eyes and made her blink.

"Someone just took a picture."

"They do that all the time. Are you ashamed to be seen with me?"

"No, but..." But what? If Bowie didn't mind having his picture taken with her, why should she mind? She should be proud to be seen with the most handsome and talented cowboy at the entire rodeo.

"Come watch my buddy Ricardo ride. I've got good seats." He took her by the hand and the crowds parted like the Red Sea as the famous Bowie West made his way through them. She found herself beaming like a celebrity as he led her across the arena to a cordoned-off section obviously reserved for VIPs.

Bowie pulled two bottles of gourmet soda from a cooler and they settled into seats so close to the arena she could practically feel the horses' breath on her face as they galloped past in the steer-roping event currently underway.

"What made you choose bull riding?"

"It's the most exciting. I've competed in all the events at some point or another, but nothing compares to staying aboard such a huge and powerful animal."

Bowie's arm brushed against hers, and she could feel the heat of his skin through his gray and green checkered shirt that brought out the color in his eyes. He glowed with excitement—as usual—and fit right in with the colorful crowd at this event.

"I don't think I've ever seen so many cowboy hats in one place. And I've spent my whole life in Texas," Lucy mused.

"Obviously you haven't spent enough of it at

rodeos," he teased. "People come from all over—Canada, Brazil, Mexico as well as all the western states."

Lucy loved how confident and masculine them men looked in their western attire, and the girls looked pretty good, too. They were everywhere, wearing tight jeans, tooled boots and shirts buttoned low to reveal enough cleavage to make a man drool.

"Hey, Bowie!" A gorgeous brunette with hair to her waist and a tall blonde in a bright red shirt waved to him from the aisle. "Good luck tonight."

"Thanks, Alyssa. You ladies looked good."

They were gone before Lucy had a chance to stare and compare herself to them unfavorably for more than a few seconds, but she couldn't help asking, "Who are they?"

"They're barrel riders. They rode a couple of days ago. I see them at a lot of events."

"Oh. Do all the barrel riders look like supermodels?"

He laughed. "I don't know. I never thought of it that way."

Now two other girls took their place, whispering and throwing shiny-eyed glances at Bowie. One of them cast a disapproving look at her. Lucy managed to smile back. Kill them with kindness, right?

"Could I get your autograph?" the taller one asked, after a few whispered exchanges.

"Sure." Bowie sprang from his seat and strode to the edge of the cordoned VIP seating. He signed their programs, and she saw one of the girls slip him a piece of paper. Lucy blinked and suppressed a gasp as he tucked it into his pocket.

19

Bowie sat down next to her again and carried on as if nothing had happened.

Lucy wrestled with her conscience for a few moments, then tried her best to sound calm. "What did she give you?"

"Probably her number." He rested his feet casually on the seat in front of him.

"You could have said no thanks." Her heart beat so fast she could hardly speak.

"That would hurt her feelings. She's not expecting me to call her. She just wanted to show off in front of her friend."

Lucy blinked. She wanted to jerk that number from Bowie's pocket and throw it away, but maybe this happened to him so often that he didn't even think about it.

Or maybe he was planning to call her later. Green talons of jealousy and insecurity clawed at her heart. "I don't like strange women giving you their number." She had to be honest. "I guess that makes me clingy."

He grinned and looked amused. "I'll dispose of it immediately." He crumpled the paper and dropped it into an empty cup on the floor. "Better?"

"A little. I guess I knew you were popular with the ladies, but it's disconcerting." Was she even his girlfriend? She was getting very territorial.

Maybe she shouldn't have come here after all. He was being friendly and gracious with his fans and now she'd made him feel bad for it.

Still, she couldn't stand to have him walking around all afternoon with another woman's number in the pocket of his jeans! Was that so unreasonable?

This was one good reason why not to ever date a famous rodeo star. Or any kind of celebrity, really. Much better to date—and marry—a quiet, hard-working man who didn't have an army of glossy-lipped fans to please.

She realized she'd crossed her arms defensively in front of her chest. Instead she should probably unbutton her shirt a little more, but that really wasn't her style. Were all these people looking at her and wondering what the great Bowie West was doing with an ordinary-looking girl like her?

Probably. Maybe they thought she was his sister. Or his third cousin twice removed. She cheered as the winner of the event was announced and managed to ask some reasonably intelligent questions about the scoring. Truth be told she couldn't wait to get out of here and be alone with Bowie again.

They had an awesome late lunch of pulled pork, and Bowie left her in the hands of two girls called Chloe and Amy when he went off to get ready for his ride. Her new companions were both barrel racers, and Amy had won some big event a couple of days ago and was basking in congratulations from almost everyone who passed.

"What brings you here?" she asked Lucy, during a

lull between events. "I know you're not on the circuit or I'd have recognized you."

"I'm here to watch Bowie," she said cryptically. She didn't feel confident enough to say that she was his girlfriend. She certainly wasn't about to share that she would be the mother of his child in a few months. She held her breath while waiting to see if Amy would press further.

"He's so handsome, isn't he? If only he could be faithful."

Lucy swallowed. "What do you mean?" As soon as she said it she knew she'd stepped onto a gangplank.

Amy tossed her long blonde hair behind her shoulder. "I suppose it's impossible to be a one-woman man when you have so many girls throwing themselves at you. At one time I thought he and I would last forever." She let out a dramatic sigh.

Lucy's blood pounded in her head. The same blood flowing through her body and into her and Bowie's baby.

Seriously? You're getting upset? You've said the same thing to yourself over and over. "So you and Bowie used to date?"

"Oh, yes. He was my first love." Amy smiled warmly, though the smile sent daggers of ice right into Lucy's heart. "There's nothing quite like that, is there?"

"Uh, no. I suppose not." She felt as if her folding chair might collapse under the weight of her sudden sadness and plunge her to the floor. But it didn't. Her life wasn't quite that dramatic. She wasn't going to ask about him cheating, though. That was none of her business.

"These bull riders are all the same. Must be

something about sitting on the back of those big, crazy beasts that makes them think the world is theirs for the taking. Oh, look, there he is now."

Lucy followed her finger, half expecting to see him lip-locked with a buxom brunette, but instead he was in the holding pen, aboard a restless black-and-white bull, wrapping the rope around his hand.

Lucy's heart clenched. She'd watched his bull riding exhibition at Jesse's but this was a whole different story. The bull was likely meaner and the results determined whether he was still in the running for the title, so whether he won or lost might decide whether he'd be happy or devastated for the rest of their time here.

She crossed her fingers quietly and whispered a tiny prayer. "Go, Bowie!" She really wanted him to win. So what if he wasn't really hers? She'd never truly dreamed he was.

"Yay, Bowie!" yelled Amy, even louder than her. "Rip it up!"

Lucy didn't want to ask what that meant in case it was some standard rodeo lingo and asking would reveal that this was indeed her first rodeo.

The timer sounded and the bull exploded out of the gate. The crowd roared as it threw a huge buck and spun, putting its back legs down almost a hundred and eighty degrees from where they'd left the ground. Bowie stayed right with the motion, one hand up in the air for balance, the other wrapped tightly to the bull's huge back.

Her blood pressure shot up as the bull darted forward and threw a huge spin in the other direction, then bucked hard, almost unseating him. Lucy let out a tiny shriek as she saw arena lights between his jeans and the bull's black-and-white back.

But he sat right back down and followed the bull as it bronced across the arena and threw its hind legs in the air one more time. The alarm sounded and Bowie jumped off and ran for the side of the arena as the crowd stood and roared.

Lucy screamed loud enough to blow a vocal chord. "You did it!" He'd be pleased with that ride. She didn't know much about bull riding but she'd done a little research and learned that it was important for the bull to throw some impressive moves. If they didn't it was the same as if a gymnast or skater executed a perfect routine that was too easy—they wouldn't get full marks. This bull had definitely thrown in the equivalent of a triple axle or two.

"He's the best, there's no denying it." Amy clapped slowly.

"You think he'll win the title?" Lucy couldn't help asking.

"He's in with a good chance. You always need luck on your side in this business." She turned and winked at Lucy. "You need the good luck to get an ornery bull and stay on it, and you need your opponents to have some bad luck at the same time."

"I could see that." Probably how it worked in love, too. If both she and Amy wanted Bowie, one of them would have to get lucky while the other got unlucky. And no doubt there was a large field of contenders for that particular prize.

"Bowie's lucky he's here riding and not behind bars on that murder charge. Pretty crazy, huh? Lucky thing his daddy has connections."

Lucy frowned. "He didn't do it."

"I never said he did." Amy smiled sweetly.

Once again Lucy was annoyed that Bowie wasn't doing more to find the real killer. Getting to this rodeo was obviously far more important to him than clearing his name.

His score popped up on the screen and she whooped with joy. "Does this mean he'll win tonight?"

"All depends on luck." Amy tossed her hair again. It had gorgeous natural looking highlights in it. Just what Lucy had been hoping for when she got hers done. "I've gotta go."

She grabbed her girlfriend and headed out to the aisle. Lucy watched her as she climbed the stands, tall, lean and obviously talented. Exactly the kind of woman she—and the fans—would expect to see Bowie West with.

Lucy glanced around, feeling at a bit of a loose end. Most of the people in the VIP area seemed to know each other well and were sitting in knots talking. She hoped Bowie would come back here, but wasn't sure if she should stay here without him. She wasn't exactly a VIP herself.

The next rider exploded into the ring on the back of a brown bull, and she sighed with relief when he fell off before the eight-second signal sounded.

She spotted Bowie on the far side of the arena, surrounded by an umbrella of cowboy hats. People held out their programs for him to sign, most of them young women in super-tight jeans and barely buttoned shirts.

"They call them buckle bunnies." A deep voice in her ear made her jump

Lucy spun around and found Jesse standing behind her. "Bowie handles the fans graciously given how annoying they can be. I didn't know you were coming." Jesse wrapped her in a big bear hug.

"Me either. It was kind of a last-minute thing. It's so exciting to see Bowie compete live."

"Yeah, almost makes me miss the game." He grinned. "But my body thanks me for getting out. And I think the horses I retrain thank me, too. Most of them would rather be cherished riding horses than crabby bucking broncs any day. The former get more treats."

"True. Are the bucking horses raised for it like bulls?"

"Not really. Most of them are just riding horses that went sour and found themselves a new career. Not exactly what their breeders and owners were hoping for but better than a pasture puff with no future, I guess." His slow grin was endearing.

"Are there horses that can't be fixed—to be ridden, I mean?"

"Maybe there are, but I haven't met one yet."

"I guess every new horse is a fresh challenge."

"Gets me out of bed every day."

Lucy wondered why Jesse wasn't married yet. He'd already settled down and had a beautiful ranch to manage and a challenging and exciting career retraining horses.

Maybe he preferred to play the field as well. "Do you miss the buckle bunnies?" she teased.

He laughed. "Not even a little bit."

She burned to ask more his romantic life—and Bowie's—but didn't want to seem intrusive or nosy.

"Let's go rescue Bowie from the ladies. He's probably dying to get out of here now that his ride is over and you're here. Let's go wait for the results with him."

Lucy grinned. At least Jesse thought Bowie would rather spend time with her than his adoring fans, and the brothers were obviously close. "I'm game. Though I hope I won't end up with claw marks on me from jealous ladies."

"You seem pretty tough." Jesse grinned. "I think you can handle them."

They picked their way across the arena, through the buzzing crowds and busy vendors. Bowie looked up just as they got there, and the smile that ripped across his face made Lucy's heart leap.

"Congratulations on your ride." She wanted to congratulate him on winning, but the event wasn't over yet. She—and no doubt everyone else—was keeping a close eye on the scoreboard after each ride. "I don't think anyone will beat you."

All eyes turned to the arena as the buzzer sounded and another ride began. The poor cowboy didn't even last four seconds, and everyone in Bowie's camp heaved a sigh of relief.

Bowie put his arm around Lucy, which sent warmth and excitement shooting through her. Three gorgeous cowgirls stared daggers at her, and she bravely smiled back. Bowie was hers right now—tonight—and she couldn't ask for anything more.

"Last one's up now, bro." Jesse nudged him as a tall cowboy in a black hat entered the ring. "This is one of Bowie's best buddies and arch rivals. Probably has the best chance of beating him, too."

A hush fell over the arena as the alarm sounded and the bull burst through the gate, bucking and spinning. Lucy gritted her teeth as the rider stayed right with him through every move, and dismounted effortlessly after the final buzzer.

Everyone's gaze shifted to the scoreboard. Since this guy and Bowie had both stayed on, the judges decision about which was a more challenging ride would decide the winner. Lucy bit her lip, hoping and praying that Bowie would have a win to celebrate with her tonight.

The score popped up—two points lower than Bowie's.

"Yes!" Jesse fist-pumped the air and everyone around Bowie cheered and high-fived him. Lucy worried for a moment that she'd get knocked to the floor in the scrum, but Bowie held tight to her the whole time.

"Don't go anywhere, Lucy. I just need to pick up my prize for today's ride, then I'll be right back and we'll find somewhere quiet to celebrate."

"Only one more good ride and the overall title is his. He's still ahead in points and only two other guys could even try to catch up with him at this point."

"When is his last ride?"

"The final day of the rodeo, of course." Jesse winked. "They don't want anyone leaving while there's still money in their pockets."

Lucy chuckled. "This is Vegas, after all. It must he hard to leave behind this kind of excitement. I can't even imagine what it would feel like to have the whole crowd roaring for you."

"It's pretty awesome, that's for sure." Jesse watched wistfully. "But life has stages and sometimes you know when it's time to move on to the next one."

"How did you know?"

"I got tired of jumping in my truck and driving a

thousand miles for a ride. I would wake up, with a big contest ahead of me and groan because I wanted to stay home with my horses."

"Also, he'd already won everything." An older man slapped Jesse on the shoulder. "These West boys are a force to be reckoned with. They'll be a lot of celebrating among the other riders when Bowie finally hangs up his spurs."

"That'll never happen," said a pretty brunette. "He's an adrenaline junkie."

"Riding bulls isn't the only way to get your adrenaline going," protested Jesse.

"It's one of the best, though." He thrust his hand at Lucy. "Clay Dawson. I taught Bowie everything he knows."

"Pleased to meet you." She smiled and shook his hand. What would Bowie's mentor and trainer think if he knew she's conceived Bowie's baby during a one-night stand? He'd probably be appalled and maybe even accuse her of trying to trap him into a dull picket-fence life he didn't want.

"Bowie's got a few good years left in him yet," Clay went on. "I'm still mad at Jesse for quitting the circuit. We all miss him."

"How do you miss me? I'm right here."

"You know what I mean. Don't you go giving your brother any ideas about quitting, you hear me?"

Jesse shrugged. "He's got his own mind."

"Drives me crazy when a boy at the peak of his career suddenly up and quits for no good reason. Especially with these million-dollar purses you all enjoy these days. No sense to it."

He gave Lucy a pointed look. She felt honored that he considered her a threat. "I enjoy watching

Bowie ride," she said innocently. No sense in mentioning that the sight of him in the back of a beast like the mythical Minotaur also gripped her with terror.

"Glad to hear it," said Clay. "Not all young ladies are so sensible."

"Clay Dawson, are you flirting with my girl?" Lucy felt Bowie's arms around her waist. She blinked, startled and thrilled that he'd claimed her so openly.

"I'm far too much of a gentleman for that," said Clay, with a wink at Lucy.

A flashbulb blinded her, and she looked up to see a photographer—possibly the only man in the whole arena not wearing a cowboy hat—taking their picture. "Smile, Bowie," called the photographer.

Bowie obliged, his arm still firmly around Lucy. She beamed a quick—and hopefully not too anxious—smile.

"Who was that?" she whispered when the photographer turned and left.

"Who knows," said Bowie. He kissed her on the cheek and she felt her skin heat under his lips. "Let's get back to my room immediately."

20

Bowie's room was right on the strip, at the Mandarin Oriental. "I stay here because it's quiet," he confessed, as they rode up in the elevator. "And I always ask for the top floor." A couple got out three floors below theirs, and Lucy gasped he seized the opportunity to push her up against the wall and kiss her with such intensity that she didn't even notice when the doors opened.

Blinking, she stepped out, still holding his hand, and he led her into a masculine suite with a view over the city. "Damn, I've missed you so much." He dropped his bag, let out a shaky breath and ran his hands over her body. "I don't think I've ever wanted to be done with a rodeo so fast before."

"Really?" It sounded like he missed her almost more than she'd missed him.

"Really." His arms wrapped around her and he kissed her so hard she could barely breathe. Her heart swelled and she knew it was filling with dangerous hope and excitement.

He's a passionate man, caught up in the moment. Don't take it too seriously.

Still...Bowie unbuttoned her shirt with trembling fingers and layered hot kisses over her breasts and chest. Then he unbuttoned her jeans and blew gently into her belly button—which did something strange to her insides and made her gasp.

She'd messed up his hair by running her hands through it, and now she struggled to get his shirt off so she could slide her fingers over all that hard muscle she'd watched in action at the arena today.

Bowie lifted her onto the bed and pulled off her boots and jeans, then buried his face between her thighs—a worshipful gesture that was so hot it made her sigh. She didn't feel at all self-conscious being naked with him. He made her feel gorgeous, sexy, totally desirable, something she'd never felt in her life before.

He kicked off his own boots, and she struggled with the button and zipper on his jeans until he took off and shucked them with breathless impatience.

His arousal was all-too obvious. "I guess we don't need a condom."

"Not that the one we used was much use anyway." He climbed over her with a sly grin. "Which was lucky. If I hadn't gotten you pregnant, you might never have called me and I didn't have your number." He sucked gently on her neck, which made her back arch. "But I'd have found you sooner or later. You are the girl next door, after all."

She laughed. "Your big ranch probably has a thousand neighbors."

"But only one that matters." Having tormented her almost to the point of madness, he entered her so slowly that she wanted to tell him to hurry.

When he finally sank all the way in, the sensation of relief was overwhelming, and she hadn't even had an orgasm yet. His lovemaking was gentle and tender at first, then faster and rougher, as her own arousal made her gasp and shriek and scratch at his back with her fingertips. She couldn't hold back for long, and climaxed with a huge shudder after only a few minutes. Bowie joined her, and she could feel his release hot inside her—powerful and primal. If she wasn't pregnant already, she'd want to be. Strange how desire—or was it love?—made her have such odd and primitive cravings.

I do love you, Bowie. Once again, she thought it but didn't say it. She'd heard warnings from an early age how letting a guy know how much you liked him was the best way to drive him away. Better for him to say it first, if he was going to.

"I'm glad you came." His voice was raspy.

"Which kind of came?" she teased.

"You can be quite a sassy young lady." He kissed her and teased her lips apart with his tongue. "Just for that I'm going to make you come again."

She glanced down. He was already growing hard.

"And this time you're going to be on top."

Lucy blinked. She'd never done any of this before. What if she was terrible and he got bored, or worse, she hurt him?

"Don't worry. It'll be fun. Just pretend I'm the bull." His wicked grin sent a shimmer of excitement through her and for a second it seemed like it actually might be fun.

"Okay," she said nervously. "Tell me if I'm doing it wrong."

He laughed and chafed her skin softly with his hands. "There's no wrong in lovemaking. If it feels good, it's right." He gestured for her to climb onto his revived erection, and she gingerly eased herself into position and sank over him. She was so aroused it was easier than she'd imagined, and the sensation of taking him deep—so deep—sent shockwaves of pleasure shooting through her.

Picturing herself riding a bull, she eased herself back and forth. First the motion was very tentative, experimental, but as heat built inside her and that mysterious flood of pleasure started up again, she began to move faster, harder, even grinding her hips a little.

She sneaked a peek at Bowie and although his eyes were closed the smile on his face let her know he was enjoying her ride.

"Woo-hoo!" she said, then giggled. She even raised her hand in the air as if she really were riding a bull, then brought it back down to run it over Bowie's deliciously hard chest.

He moved his hips in time with hers and soon the feelings flooding through her became so overwhelming and intense that she knew she was heading for another climax.

Emotion built inside her at the same time. Her feelings for Bowie were getting stronger every day, and physical intimacy only reinforced the connection forming between them. Truth be told, she was totally crazy about him.

She let out a cry as her orgasm tore through her, and felt Bowie tense up as his own climax hit him at the same time. She gasped and collapsed forward onto him, where she lay there panting softly against his neck.

"Ride 'em, cowgirl." Bowie's voice was rich with amusement.

"I think I just did." Hers was barely a whisper. "I

stayed on longer than eight seconds, too."

Bowie's chest shook with laughter. "You were awesome."

"Was I?" The whole experience was so new, so strange. The intense pleasure of sex took her by surprise. She knew people made a big fuss out of it, but until she met Bowie she had no idea why.

She eased herself off him and lay beside him, their faces cheek to cheek.

He stroked her hair, and kissed her lips gently. "Yes. I consider myself very lucky that you saved yourself for me all these years."

She knew he was teasing. "I didn't mean to be a virgin at twenty-seven. It just kind of happened. Or rather, it didn't happen. Dating a guy who was secretly gay for four years didn't help either. I should really have been more suspicious. He kept saying he wanted to wait until he was married."

"To another man."

"Exactly. I was his convenient cover story and he'd have strung me along for years if he hadn't finally come out. I thought he was a close friend, but he vanished right out of my life after that admission. Makes it harder than ever to trust anyone."

She wanted to ask if Bowie ever thought about marriage. She was curious just to hear what he thought about the idea of two people spending their lives together. But there was no way she could ask.

He'd assume she was talking about the two of them and putting pressure on him. Which she totally wasn't. Putting pressure on Bowie would probably cause him to launch out of her life like a rocket.

He frowned, then she felt his chest swell against hers as he inhaled. "What do you think about marriage, Lucy?"

Lucy blinked. Had Bowie just asked exactly the question she was thinking? Her heart started pounding and she knew he could probably feel it.

"I don't know. I mean, when I was little I always dreamed of getting married one day and having a big, white wedding, but my parents got divorced when I was sixteen and there was a nasty custody battle over pretty much everything so that kind of soured me on marriage."

Phew! She'd managed to say something that didn't put any pressure on him at all. Besides, she really wasn't looking to get married. She had a full life with friends and her boarders and all her horses.

She also had no problem being a single mother, though she did want their child to have a relationship with his father. See how cool she was? She didn't even feel clingy, let alone act it.

Of course, who didn't want to live happily ever after with the man of her dreams, but she wasn't going to hold her breath waiting for that to happen.

Bowie's frown had deepened. "I guess you're right. Marriage doesn't work out too often these days. My parents were married right up until my mom's death five years ago. They still adored each other, which I suppose is pretty rare. Especially since my dad is such an ornery old cuss no one else can stand him."

"I bet he's lonely now."

"No one else to blame but himself. You don't win people's love by trying to control them."

"True." Lucy congratulated herself again for her hands-off approach to Bowie. "But maybe attempting to exert control his way of showing love?"

"I doubt it. My lawyer asked me if my dad could

be involved in framing me for the murder. I told him no, just like I told you before, but he wanted to dig deeper."

"Why?"

"When they brought Dad's foreman in for questioning, Crane wondered if maybe my dad had hired him to kill the victim. The foreman's tire prints were found near the scene. Apparently, one of them had a nail in it that made it distinctive."

"Was he arrested?"

"Nope. They let him go due to lack of evidence."

She struggled to process the information. "Because he planned the whole thing and planted evidence accusing you."

"Exactly. That's what I think, anyway. The DA's office still hasn't formally dropped the charges against me. My lawyer says the only surefire way to make them do that is to find the real killer and get him convicted."

"Do you think your dad could be behind it?"

Bowie shook his head and blew out a long breath. "No. He isn't my number-one fan, but I can't think of one good reason why he'd want to get me accused of murder."

"You said he was trying to buy the land back from you."

"Sure, but it's just land. He's got plenty already. Besides, putting me in jail or the electric chair doesn't give it back to him. I could leave it to one of my brothers. As far as I can guess the foreman did it, but I have no idea why."

Lucy hugged him close, drinking in the warm, masculine scent of him. "If we hadn't made love that night…" She bit her lip. She hadn't intended to use the dreaded L-word. "If I hadn't become pregnant, you might have been convicted already."

"Tell me about it. The hand of fate moves in mysterious ways." He stroked her belly with his broad hand. "It's lucky for me that you did get pregnant."

Lucky for me, too. Strange how her views on the situation were shifting. What had first seemed like terrible bad luck—to get pregnant on your very first time—had brought Bowie well and truly into her life. If she wasn't pregnant who knows if he ever would have fit her into his busy schedule again.

"We should have dinner. Is there somewhere you'd like to go? If there's a show you want to see I know a guy who can get last-minute tickets to pretty much anything. We can do whatever you want."

I know what I want. "Can we order room service?"

A slow grin spread across his face. "Why, yes, we can."

Lucy's eyes cracked open just as morning sunlight started to creep around the blackout curtains. She stirred slightly and enjoyed the weight of Bowie's big arm across her chest. "I guess I should have brought a change of clothes with me. I'll have to drive back to my hotel."

"I have to get to the arena early this morning. I promised a reporter I'd do an interview."

She sighed. "I guess we'll have to go our separate ways for a while. And maybe I should catch up on some sleep, too." It had been a fun but rather exhausting night. "Will you have enough energy to ride today?"

"I always have enough energy, sweetheart." His soft kiss made her lips tingle, and the endearment made her heart swell with joy. "You give me energy. I'll call you when I'm done and we'll spend the day together. If I make it through today's ride—"

"Which you will."

"I do plan to." He winked. "Then the final ride is tomorrow."

"So you do need a good night's sleep tonight."

"Don't you worry about me. I got more sleep last night than I've had in some entire weeks. I used to be quite wild when I was younger."

She chuckled. From what she'd read, that was pretty recent.

"But before you go, I'd like some breakfast."

"Room service again?"

"I had something slightly different in mind." His mouth lowered over her nipple and stirred a flurry of sensations in parts of her body she barely knew existed until she met Bowie.

"You are tireless." *Me too.* She couldn't believe how fast he aroused her each time. She wove her fingers into his hair as he circled his tongue around her nipple so gently it made her shiver, then sucked it hard enough to make her hips buck.

After another exhilarating lovemaking session— she was making up for her late start—they called room service for a huge breakfast of eggs, bacon and all the works, and enjoyed it under the covers.

"Are you ever tempted to spend your entire day in bed, calling room service to cater to all your needs?" He was rich enough.

"Nope. Too restless." His face creased into a smile. "I always want to get out there and do something."

He stroked her cheek softly, which softened the

reminder that Bowie was the proverbial rolling stone. He'd rest for a while, but then he couldn't wait to get going again. "Me too, I guess. I really should call the ranch and see how all the horses are doing. Stevie's probably done with the feed shift by now." She groped around on the nightstand for her phone.

"Sounds good. I'm going to hit the shower."

With one last, lingering kiss, they headed their separate ways. Bowie for an interview at the Thomas and Mack center, and her back to her far less fabulous hotel.

She showered and changed, then felt at a loose end. According to Stevie, everything was going smoothly back at High Pastures. She decided to drive back to the strip, park, and walk around a little. Bowie might already be done with his interview, but she resolved to wait for him to call her. She's surprised him by arriving yesterday, and he might have had plans in place already for today.

She walked around for about twenty minutes, then the heat started to get to her so she decided to step into a sports bar and buy a lemonade and some nachos. The waitress was setting down her plate when she saw a familiar face appear on a screen on the far side of the room—Bowie.

The TV nearest her had some golf tournament playing. "Can we switch this TV to that channel?" She pointed across the room.

"Sure, I'll take care of it." The waitress hurried back to the bar, and sure enough Bowie appeared right over Lucy's head. The banner behind him was from the Thomas and Mack center, so this was likely the interview he'd left for this morning.

"—now, you would have probably been higher in

the rankings this year if you hadn't missed the event in Amarillo. Your rivals gained some points on you there. You were behind bars at that point, right?"

"I was falsely accused of a crime I didn't commit."

"You haven't been fully exonerated, though, have you?"

"Not yet, but I'm confident that I will be."

"You were spotted here yesterday with the lady who came forward as your alibi, Lucy Neel."

Lucy cringed as a big shot of her—shiny-faced and grimacing at the camera—appeared on the screen. This must be from last night, when the photographer took their picture. She glanced around the bar, hoping no one realized it was her. So the story about his alibi had got out, at least to this reporter.

"Yes, she came here to watch me ride." That sexy, lazy grin spreading across his mouth made her feel all warm inside.

"So you two are still an item?"

"Absolutely."

Lucy felt a smile rip across her mouth.

"She's having your baby."

Her smile vanished.

"Yes." Bowie looked more serious. "We are having a baby together."

"So Bowie West is finally settling down. If you win the title this year, will you quit the circuit?"

"Too early to tell." His warm grin reappeared.

Lucy stared. She'd been sure he'd say no. Was there really a chance that he would quit the circuit and settle down with her—maybe even start breeding bulls on his vast ranch that was oh-so-conveniently right next to hers? With that much land at their disposal, maybe she could even start breeding horses.

She'd always dreamed of doing that but—

"We recorded this interview earlier this morning and since I sat down with Bowie West, some startling news has come to light." She snapped out of her reverie as a young, male reporter with shiny white teeth faded to a picture of the murder victim, Terri Balboa. "The woman Bowie West was accused of shooting had few friends and no known relatives, but one of them has come forward. She claims she was there with Bowie and Terri on the night of the murder, and that she spent time with them before that fateful night."

21

Lucy's mouth dropped open as a picture of an overly tanned blonde in a red tank top appeared on the screen. "Kelly Clifford told reporters this morning that she became close to the bull riding star over the last few months when he would spend time with her and Terri at Terri's apartment in Aileen, Texas. She was spotted in Vegas with him earlier this week."

Her heart pounded as she watched a new picture appear. The same girl, now almost spilling out of a low-cut bustier, with her arms wrapped around a smiling Bowie's neck. "This picture was taken just two days ago and suggests that Bowie had more of a relationship with the murder victim than he's let on. Kelly spoke to our reporter a few minutes ago. 'Oh, I love Bowie far too much to ever testify against him. I can't tell you what happened later on that night. I wasn't there. All I know is that Bowie and Terri were close and it ain't right of him to pretend like he never knew her.'"

"Can I get you any—" The waitress's voice in her ear startled Lucy so much that she spilled her lemonade all over the table. In the intervening fuss of mopping it up and apologizing she missed the reporter's next comments. When she glanced back up at the screen they'd moved onto a story about the number-two-ranked bull rider in the contest.

"Are you okay, sweetie?" The waitress looked concerned.

"Yes, fine. Just fine. The check, please." Lucy couldn't believe it. Not only had Bowie lied to her about not knowing the murder victim, he'd been intimate with her best friend two days ago!

The reporter had been talking while the waitress interrupted, but she caught his final comment. "Bowie West can ride a mean bull but will his love of the ladies be his undoing? After all, a bull has no fury like a woman scorned." His laugh added insult to injury.

Was she the "woman scorned"? She certainly had some fury rolling in her veins right now.

She pulled her phone out of her purse with shaking hands and dialed his number. "Hi, sexy mama, how are you?"

"What?" She could hardly believe he'd pretend like this hadn't happened. "Did you see the television story about you?"

"No, I avoid those things like the plague." He laughed. Then there was a pause. "What did they say?"

Lucy struggled to keep her breathing under control. Maybe he did sneak out of her room that night and go murder that woman. He'd certainly climbed out of bed and got dressed before she woke up. He only woke her to say goodbye. He could have disappeared for an hour or two then come back and said goodbye. Maybe even drugged her so she wouldn't wake up....

Her hand was trembling so much she could barely

hold her phone. "They said," she tried to whisper so no one in the bar would hear. "That you did know Terri—" She didn't want to say the name. "The victim. They showed you with her best friend."

"What?"

"You were with her this week, here in Vegas. There was a PBR banner right behind you in the picture."

"I was with who?"

"The girl." She couldn't remember her name. "A hot blonde. I guess they all run together after a while."

"But I wasn't. I don't know who they're talking about. I never met Terri Balboa."

Lucy's heart sank. Somewhere deep inside her she hoped he'd have a convincing explanation. This wasn't it. "She said you were all friends. That you hung out together."

"And you believe her?"

Lucy bit her lip. "I don't know what to believe."

"I'm used to people making up stories about me. I barely pay attention anymore. That's all this is."

"But you could have—" The waitress appeared with her check so she bent her head down. "You could have left my bedroom that night. I was asleep. And the murder wasn't all that far away."

Cold fingers of dread clawed at her heart as she accused the man she loved of murder.

His response was a distressing moment of silence.

"Do you really think I could do that?"

She swallowed. "I don't want to think that, but I don't really know you that well, do I? The pregnancy put our relationship in fast-forward so maybe I didn't stop to ask myself the tough questions." She felt tears rising. "For years I watched my dad lie to my mom. He told her he was working late, that he was holding a youth group meeting, that he was comforting a parishioner—and he was cheating on her the whole time. He had affairs with at least eight women while they were married. He told those lies like he really believed them, and for a long time, my mom believed them too."

"I wouldn't lie to you."

"No? How do I know that's not a lie? My dad was very charming, too." A tiny sob squeaked out of her. She tried to hold back tears while she thrust her credit card and the check at the waitress. "He fooled everyone. Then when my mom figured it out, she didn't want to break up our family so she kept it to herself."

"Lucy, I'm not your dad."

"No. You're a lot better looking than him, and famous and way richer. And you've probably slept with more women that he did, too, because of that. And right now I can't trust you."

"What can I do to make you trust me?"

A tear fell on the shiny oak table as the waitress brought her card back and she signed the check. The poor waitress looked alarmed. "I don't know. Maybe I can't ever trust anyone. Maybe that's why I avoided relationships for so long." A shaky sob left her. Now she was blaming herself! That's not why she called him.

"Who did murder Terri Balboa, Bowie?" She raised her voice enough so that the people at the next table turned to stare. "And why aren't you trying harder to find out?"

She grabbed her stuff and hurried outside into the

midday heat. "You've been hiding out comfortably at my ranch and not putting too much effort into finding the culprit. Is your dad's ranch foreman a convenient smokescreen that the mighty West family cooked up to spring you from jail so you could compete in the big rodeo?"

Conspiracy theories unfurled in her mind. "I know that rich and powerful men don't feel the rules apply to them. Heck, my dad wasn't even rich and powerful and he sure felt that way. Who killed her, Bowie? And why does her best friend claim to know you?"

"I'm not sure what's going on, but I need to find out. My dad's foreman is still running the ranch so I'm going to go talk with him right now."

Lucy almost dropped her phone. "But what about the rodeo? Your final ride is tomorrow."

"Tomorrow is another day. Today, I need to prove to you that I'm neither a killer nor a liar."

She wasn't sure what to say next, but she didn't have to say anything, because he'd hung up. Lucy stood in the middle of the wide sidewalk on the strip, sun baking down on her and people pushing past her in both directions.

This morning she'd woken up so happy in Bowie's arms. In a few short minutes the whole fairy castle future she'd built in her head—breeding horses on *his* ranch land!—had crumbled to dust with the realization that she might even be an unwitting accessory to murder as well as a first-class dupe.

Maybe she should head right back home. But then she'd have to face Val and all those sympathetic and consoling faces of her boarders. No doubt they knew from the start that a man like Bowie West couldn't truly be interested in her if she weren't his alibi.

Tears flowed freely down her face. It had felt so real. The sensations and emotions that roared through her when Bowie was around had her truly convinced that she was in love with him.

Maybe it was her inexperience showing. At least they weren't face-to-face right now. She'd probably have fallen into his arms after one look from those flashing green eyes. She couldn't believe that he'd had that blonde woman's arms around him this very week. Even if there was no murder involved at all, that was enough to send her running for cover.

Her heart ached. Maybe a long-distance relationship with someone who'd never, ever love you wasn't so awful after all. It certainly never left her feeling this devastated and adrift.

Bowie booked a flight back to Austin and drove to the airport without even returning to his hotel room. He kept his temper while calling the reporter who'd interviewed him, then run the story—pointing out that he never heard of Kelly Clifford—and learned that she'd approached them.

Within ninety minutes he was on a plane and by mid afternoon he was driving up the long, tree-lined drive to his least favorite place on earth.

The Old West Ranch, as they half-jokingly called it, had been built with the blood, sweat and tears of his ancestors and the countless people they'd oppressed and exploited in their path to domination of the entire region. The Big House—again, only half joking—was a grim Gothic affair built during the robber baron era when oil and railroads had turned the family fortunes from wealthy to ridiculously rich.

He hadn't phoned ahead. He wanted the element

of surprise on his side. The ranch foreman didn't know him from Adam since he gave this place as wide a berth as possible, and hadn't been back here in years.

His father hated him for ruining the family reputation at their traditional boarding school, refusing to learn the oil business, and leading his younger—and arguably more talented—brother Jesse astray into the bull riding world.

His dad now lived here with his youngest brother, Shane, and a crew of loyal servants who waited on him hand and foot. One of them hurried toward him now.

"May I help you?" The middle-aged man with the beer belly eyed his mud-spattered truck with suspicion.

"I'm here to see Russell Jenkins."

"Why?" The man's eyes narrowed.

"I have my reasons." Bowie raised himself up to his full height and looked down on the man. "Mr. Jenkins, I presume."

"Who are you?" Jenkins asked rudely.

"My name is Bowie West."

Jenkins frowned, and a look of panic entered his watery blue eyes. "What do you want with me?"

"For starters, I'd like to know why you broke into my loft, stole my gun, planted some strange woman's possessions there, had her call me, then killed her and tried to frame me for the crime." Bowie kept his voice and demeanor steady.

"I did none of those things."

"What I can't figure out is *why* you did them." Bowie crossed his arms. "That has me perplexed."

Jenkins blinked rapidly. "You can't prove a thing."

"No? You made sure of that, huh? Then it was premeditated." Bowie glanced up at the imposing stone house, with its ornamental turrets, and sucked in a breath. "Did my dad put you up to it?"

Jenkins screwed up his face. "I'm no contract killer. No matter what's gone on between you and your father, it's none of my business."

Bowie frowned. "I know he wants the land I inherited."

"He's got plenty of land."

"Having plenty of something has never stopped a West from wanting more." Bowie didn't know which of them was more likely to be behind it. "Where did you find Kelly Clifford?"

Jenkins's startled reaction was a dead giveaway. "Who?" His attempted cover sounded totally unconvincing.

"Someone paid her to make up nonsense about knowing me. It was either you or my dad or the both of you together."

"What do I have against you? I've never even met you."

So he was trying to pin it on his boss. Bowie himself couldn't see what this man would have against him, but then why would his dad want him accused of murder? That was more tarnish on the family name and didn't make sense either.

"I don't think this is about me at all." Bowie looked at Jenkins through narrowed eyes. "I think it's about Terri Balboa, and I'm just a convenient scapegoat."

Jenkins's mouth opened. Then closed.

"You knew her. Several witnesses have said that."

"So did you."

"Ah, but I didn't." Bowie cocked his head. "You might try to convince others that I did, even making up a reason for her to call my phone several times, but I know that I've never met her. I never even heard of her until I was accused of murdering her. The only thing I don't understand is why you're walking around free."

"No evidence." Jenkins lifted his chin and a nasty smirk tugged at the corners of his lips. "Whereas her belongings were found in your home."

"Because you planted them there."

"I don't know what you're talking about." Jenkins gaze hardened. So he planned to brazen this thing out, confident that he'd covered his tracks well enough that neither the police nor the prosecutor could pin anything on him.

And he'd done a good job. Bowie's lawyer had hired a team to comb through his phone records, and there was not a single call to Terri Balboa. He must have used a disposable phone for his dealings with her. And the security camera over the door on Bowie's loft building had conveniently been out of service for a month.

Bowie was pretty sure that the man before him was the murderer who framed him and put him behind bars, and his adrenaline spiked as the prospect of punching that smirk off Jenkins' face flashed through his mind.

But that would only be playing into his hands.

Bowie stared at him for a long, hard moment, then continued walking toward the big gray house.

"Where are you going?" called Jenkins, bravado sounding hollow in his voice.

"To dive into the bosom of my family."

Two unfamiliar men in expensive-looking suits came down the front steps as he approached, and he heard his brother Shane, who always looked tall, handsome, and elegant as a forties matinée idol, murmuring goodbye to them in businesslike tones. He stared when he saw Bowie.

"What are you doing here?"

"Enjoying the warm hospitality." Bowie glanced sideways at the suited men, as they climbed into a large black Mercedes sedan. "And you?"

"You know what I'm doing here."

"Being a chip off the old block."

"Running the family business. Something none of the rest of you can be bothered with." Shane's gray eyes were hard to read. He never seemed angry at being left to shoulder the burden. He didn't seem entirely thrilled about it, either.

Bowie, Jesse and Daniel had once asked him how he felt about them all heading off to pursue their dreams and leaving him holding the keys to the filing cabinet, and he avoided giving a real answer. Shane should have been a poker player.

But then the oil business probably wasn't all that different from poker and likely there was more money in it.

"Where's Dad?" Bowie glanced around, not really wanting to be surprised by the old man, who could be mean as a rattler.

"In the Caymans."

"Wining and dining girls half his age and tending the offshore money farms?"

"Something like that. Would you like a coffee?"

Bowie grinned. "Now this is the kind of hospitality I'm talking about. I'd like one very much."

Soon he and Shane were sharing a lunch of roast chicken and vegetables prepared by the cook. When they'd shared enough pleasantries about the state of old homestead (expensive to keep up) and the state of the family oil business (better than ever), Bowie decided it was time to get down to business. "Why does Dad want my land back so much that he's offering me an arm and a leg for it. It's only five thousand acres and it's not like the area is going to become a suburb of Austin any time soon."

"You know why. Oil in the sands."

"Fracking will ruin that whole valley."

Shane kept his poker face firmly intact. "There are methods of containing the contamination."

Bowie snorted. "Sure there are. And maybe you can turn it into a beach resort while you're at it. I'll never sell."

"Why?" Shane looked genuinely curious. "You never even go near it. And it's leased out for way less than market value. Why do you care what happens to it?"

"I've become friendly with my next-door neighbor. She runs a horse farm. She's made me appreciate the beauty of the place. I think I'm going to raise some bucking bulls there."

To Bowie's surprise a broad smile started to spread across Shane's face. "You, raising animals?"

"Why not?"

"Why not indeed." The poker mask descended again. "Don't worry about Dad. He's like a Jack Russell terrier and can't stand to hear the word *no*, but he's got other projects on the front burner now."

"So he's not going to try to frame me for another murder and put me out of the picture in the county jail." He stared hard at Shane, despite his joking tone.

His brother looked shocked. "You don't think he did that?"

"I don't know what to think."

Shane shook his head and blew out hard. "Never. Dad takes the family business very seriously. And the family. Why would he want a West behind bars?"

"That's what I thought." He frowned. "But why is that foreman still working here? Isn't he the prime suspect now?"

Shane shook his head. "It's a storm in a teacup. It'll be forgotten in six months."

"Because no one cares about a dead hooker."

Shane shrugged. "Russell Jenkins is a good foreman. It's not easy to manage multiple properties with a mix of oil and ranching operations."

"Business as usual." Bowie put his napkin on the table. "Can't say I'm surprised." He stood up and stretched. The atmosphere in this house always seemed to suck the wind out of him. And he had one more place to visit this afternoon.

"It was good to see you." Shane's warm expression appeared genuine.

Probably a trick of the light. "Yeah, bro. Take care of yourself. And thanks for lunch." He headed for the door as fast as he could without breaking into a run.

22

Bowie pulled up in front of the Half Moon Café, a dingy dive just a short crawl from a rest stop where truckers could park for the night. This was not the kind of café where you could get a sustainably grown cappuccino. As he approached the battered door he could hear mournful country music.

A tall woman with makeup spackled onto a lean face welcomed him with a smile as he entered. "What can I get you, cowboy?"

"The truth." He pulled up a barstool. "Have you ever seen me before?"

The barmaid squinted at him, her false eyelashes moving like spiders' legs. "You do look a mite familiar."

Great. That's what came of being a "famous" rodeo cowboy. "I mean, have you ever seen me in this bar before."

Heels clicked across the floor toward him and a velvet voice accosted him from behind. "If you'd ever been in this dump before I'd remember it."

He turned to see a petite brunette with a truly enormous bust and a hard expression on her pretty face.

"You're sure about that."

"Yep." The brunette lit a cigarette and blew out the smoke. "I know who you are. You're Bowie West. I spend all my days and nights in this pleasure palace, since I own it, and I know for sure that you have never been here."

Relief flooded him. "Thank you."

"That's where I recognize you from. The news stories." The barmaid leaned toward him, resting her elbows on the bar and giving him a view of wrinkled cleavage. "I never watch those rodeos. Waste of a good cowboy."

He managed a wry smile. "You aren't the only one to feel that way. I'm cutting out on a big rodeo right now because I need to prove to someone that I didn't murder Terri Balboa."

"We know you didn't, sweetheart." The brunette tapped her ash in an ashtray next to his hand. "My suspicions rest on that high and mighty Russell Jenkins. Not that anyone asked us."

"The police didn't interview you?"

"Nope." They spoke in unison.

"What the hell?" He stood up. "Something is really fishy here. What makes you think he did it?"

"Just makes sense." The brunette frowned and blew smoke at the ceiling. "He wanted to stop paying for Terri's time. She liked the idea of quitting the business and settling down, so she went along with it for a while. When she realized he had no intention of making an honest woman of her and she'd just been giving it away for nothing, she got real mad and demanded back-pay."

"And he told her she wasn't worth a dime more than he'd already give her," finished the barmaid. "She told us this herself. She was upset because she had no money for rent. She thought he would ask her to live with him at the ranch."

"So she said she was going to go to his employer and…I don't know what she thought would come of that." The brunette shook her head and blew out a plume of smoke. "I doubt she'd ever have done it anyway. She was on fire to get revenge then she got distracted by a letter saying she'd won some prize drawing that was probably a scam. Kept calling and calling to get her money. Thought she was going to retire and live happily ever after." She frowned. "And two days later she turned up dead."

"We figured it was him." The barmaid shook her head.

"And you didn't go to the police?" Bowie was incredulous.

"Sweetheart, we're not exactly running a Dairy Queen here. We don't have the most warm and intimate relationship with the local sheriff."

Bowie glanced at their scanty attire and nodded. "I see. But if you were asked to testify, would you tell the truth?"

"For you, sweetheart, I'd do almost anything."

"Do you know this woman?" He pulled up a picture of Kelly Clifford on his phone.

They both frowned at it. "Can't say I do. Is she local?"

"I don't know. Supposedly she and I were hanging out with Terri Balboa some time before her murder."

"Listen, my darling, Terri spent as much of her time here as we do. If you were in her life, or if this woman was, we'd have known about it."

"Thanks. I really appreciate your candor." He was tempted to leave a big tip, then thought better of it.

He didn't want to be accused of buying their testimony. Instead he looked ruefully around the empty bar. "I hope business picks up, ladies."

"You and me both," said the owner. "Murder is bad for business."

Since the local police were obviously in someone's pocket—or at the very least, dangerously incompetent—Bowie decided to share his newly gained information with the press and his lawyer rather than the sheriff's office. And he waited to do that until he was safely on the ten o'clock flight back to Austin.

Lucy sat alone in her hotel room, surfing the Internet and flipping through the channels on the TV. Now Bowie might miss his big championship ride tomorrow and it would be her fault. She probably should have just butted out.

She knew he wasn't really hers, anyway.

If people on the streets of Vegas tonight knew that she was the reason the number-one-ranked bull rider was MIA, she'd probably be run out of town on a rail.

She hesitated every time she reached the local news station, hoping for a breaking update on the story—and dreading it in the same breath. What if Bowie got arrested again? Why had she believed a smooth-talking news reporter over the man who'd awakened her fearful heart?

It was all her fault. She probably wasn't capable of the kind of trust a relationship required. And guilt and regret were proving to be really annoying roommates in her cramped "suite." There wasn't even room to pace around the bed without tripping over her bag and boots.

For the thirty-seventh time that hour her fingers hovered over her phone, wanting to call him and at least make sure he'd be back in time.

A knock on the door made her jump. "Who is it?"

"Bowie."

She blinked. Should she let him in like nothing had happened?

Yes.

She hurried to the door, stepping over her bag on the way, and opened it. His broad shoulders blocked her doorway and his hat shadowed his face.

Her heart filled with joy. "You made it back in time."

Or maybe he never went anywhere.

Doubts crowded her mind as she took in his serious expression. "What happened?"

"I haven't had time to figure out exactly who Kelly Clifford is and how she plays into this—though I remind you I've never seen her before." He held his chin high, as if talking to a jury rather than a lover. "But I flew back to Aileen and talked to Terri's closest friends and they've never heard of her either. She came out of nowhere. I also questioned Russell Jenkins, the foreman, and he seems guilty as sin, so as soon as I can figure out how to link the two of them together—"

Lucy couldn't stand it any longer. "I'm so sorry." Her lip quivered. "I shouldn't have doubted you."

"Oh, yes, you should. As you said, you don't know me that well."

"Innocent until proven guilty. That's how it's supposed to be..." Her thoughts were jumbled. She wanted so badly to take him in her arms and kiss him.

But he stood there, rigid and formal, in the dim

light of the hallway outside her bedroom. "But that's not how it really plays out, is it?" He let out a sigh. "You were absolutely right that I needed to take this into my own hands. Can you believe the police never even questioned Terri's friends?"

"Why not?"

"Because they're strippers and hookers so everything they say is a lie." He shrugged. "Everyone's a villain in this story. Including me, I guess. I don't blame you for thinking I knew that woman. She was hanging all over me in that picture, which was taken this week. I'm so used to women crushing around me that I barely notice it." His green eyes glinted, but not with the usual mischief, more a hint of recrimination. "And my reputation as a playboy is well deserved."

Lucy swallowed. "That doesn't make you a killer."

"My lawyer says the police and the DA's office aren't taking the new story too seriously, so I can ride tomorrow."

"Thank goodness."

"And I'd like you to be there."

"Of course! That's why I flew to Vegas." Would it be so wrong if she took one step forward and gave him a hug?

"Well then," he hesitated for a moment and touched the brim of his hat. "I'll see you tomorrow. Be sure to sit in the VIP area so I can find you." Then he bowed his head slightly and left.

Lucy stood there, watching his tall, muscular frame move down the hallway. She wanted desperately to call out, "Stop!" but she didn't dare.

Maybe he didn't want to be with her. She'd betrayed his trust by doubting him. Would she want to sleep with someone who'd believed—even for one split second—that she could be a killer?

She resolved to try to sleep, and tomorrow she'd be at the arena, yelling louder than anyone else, when Bowie rode for the big prize.

23

Lucy woke up the next morning to a local news report filled with excitement about the finals and—to her immense relief—an exposé of Kelly Clifford as a convicted shoplifter, streetwalker and small-time con artist. She even tearfully admitted that she'd been paid to get in a picture with Bowie but that the man who paid her was rich and powerful and she feared for her life so she couldn't say his name.

Lucy rolled her eyes. She doubted the foreman at the West ranch was that rich and powerful, but whatever.

She noticed with a start that Bowie was now number two in the rankings. He'd missed a round yesterday that had given a boost to some of his opponents' cumulative scores.

It's your fault. She cursed herself for doubting him. Still, none of that would matter if he had the best ride today, would it?

She itched to call him but settled for a text: "Good luck today!"

As soon as she'd sent it she decided that it was totally lame and impersonal and just proved how hopelessly unworthy she was of his affections—which had probably now moved onto someone else, anyway.

Still, she set off for the arena bright and early, with anticipation humming in her veins. She expected resistance, velvet ropes and red tape at the entrance to the VIP arena, but to her surprise she was welcomed in, and Jesse waved her over to sit next to him.

She sat down gingerly. "Is he really mad at me?"

"Mad?" Jesse frowned. "Why would he be mad at you?"

"Because—" She hesitated. Bowie clearly hadn't told Jesse that she'd taken a reporter's word over his and missed a day of the rodeo chasing after the truth. Maybe he wouldn't want his brother to know how little she trusted him. "I'm nervous about him riding." The fib felt thick on her tongue.

"Nervous about Bowie? He could ride an exploding volcano and fall off feet first. Don't worry about him." Jesse's warm brown eyes encouraged her to relax and enjoy the spectacle—thousands of cowboys and cowgirls milling around enjoying the biggest bull-riding event of the year.

"Will he be really upset if he doesn't win?"

"No more upset than last year." Jesse winked. "Or the year before that when I beat him. Losing is part of the game."

"But this is the closest he's ever come to winning, isn't it?"

"Yep. But I'm not so sure he wants to win." Jesse sighed. The first rider was mounting his bull inside the pen, and the crowd grew louder than ever in anticipation.

"What do you mean?"

"If he wins, then everyone will expect him to quit while he's ahead, and I don't think he's ready to do that. If he doesn't win, he has the perfect excuse to keep riding and running around the country."

Lucy nodded sagely. Not exactly a surprise. Even Bowie's own brother didn't think he wanted to settle down yet. "You think he'd get bored with ranching."

"No, I didn't say that." Jesse's eyes flashed with indignation. "I think he'd love it. Ranching is filled with all different kinds of challenges to keep you on your toes." He shrugged. "I just don't know if he's ready to stand still long enough to try it. Bowie's always lived his life eight seconds at a time.

The first rider got thrown almost immediately, and a moan rose from the crowd. By the time they got the first bull out of the arena, the second rider was up on his bull, and the gate exploded open. Lucy grimaced as he got tossed around like a rag doll before finally giving up his grip on the rope.

"If anything could settle him down, it's probably you having a baby."

"That wasn't exactly planned," she admitted.

"Most of the best things aren't." His warm grin told her he didn't blame her. "I'm looking forward to being an uncle."

Lucy smiled. "Uncle Jesse has a nice ring to it. I think you might need to get a corncob pipe."

Jesse chuckled. "I'll get a rocker for my porch, too."

The third rider stayed on for about five seconds, just long enough for Lucy to get nervous, before he bit the dirt.

Again Lucy wanted to ask Jesse why he wasn't married. He wasn't even dating anyone from what she could tell. Surely if he was, she'd be here today. With looks and money like his, there couldn't be any shortage of offers. "Do you think you'll have kids one day?" That seemed a low-pressure way to ask about his personal life.

"I'd like to." He never took his eyes off the next rider, who had the bad luck of a dull bull who didn't put much effort into the whole endeavor. The rider stayed on but she knew his score wouldn't be impressive. "But I'm very happy with my life as it is right now."

"As well you should be. Your ranch is so beautiful. And you have enough baby bulls and other people's misbehaving horses to keep you busy."

They chattered about the area, and her plans for her place, Lucy blabbing on to keep her nerves steady. She caught occasional glimpses of Bowie down near the bull pen. Or glimpses of the top of his hat, anyway.

"Only one more rider before Bowie." Jesse stretched and cracked his knuckles. "I'm more nervous than if I was riding myself."

"Bowie doesn't seem the type to get nervous."

"Oh, we all try our best to look cool, but on the inside we're all humming." He sighed as the rider sat through a pretty impressive broncing session. "He's going to need a really good ride to climb to the top of this scoreboard."

Lucy held her breath and knotted her fingers together as Bowie climbed aboard a huge black bull. The announcer pointed out that this bull was ranked number one and should give a challenging ride. Lucy knew she should be happy about this—more chance of a high points ride—but the high ranking also meant that the bull was the most dangerously hard to ride bull in the arena tonight.

If Bowie won today, all his hard work would pay

off and he could spend a lifetime celebrating the highest achievement bull riding had to offer and a cool million to add to his coffers. The big win would also make his recent legal troubles—and the contests they'd caused him to miss—fade into obscurity. Heck, maybe he'd even retire and enjoy the good life.

His white straw hat shone against the bull's black coat as she watched him wind the rope around his hand.

If he lost, he'd probably have to keep chasing the title, following the circuit, and risking his neck for another year—or more.

Please win, Bowie!

She wanted the bull to give an impressive attempt at getting him off and for him to ride it safely. It was a lot to ask for.

Even Jesse's big strong hands wrapped over the rail in front of them, knuckles turning pale as he fixed his gaze on his brother.

The whistle sounded and the bull burst out of the gate. It leapt forward and spun three times in one direction. Spinning was good, right? Bowie held fast as it dived down, then shot forward like a fired bullet.

Lucy wanted to close her eyes. How far along were they? Three seconds? Four?

The bull spun the other way, then dived again and bucked so huge that she saw Bowie fly forward.

His hat hit the ground crown first. "Oh, no—" The words left her lips as his denim-clad butt left the bull's back and his free hand shot higher in the air. Somehow he managed to get down on the bull's back again, and even spurred the bull as it spun across the arena.

I'm getting dizzy just watching. She gripped the rail in

front as if holding on tight could help Bowie stay in position. Her blood pounded in her brain, drowning out the roar of the crowd.

The bull threw in one more three-buck fit before the buzzer sounded. Bowie jumped clear and grabbed his hat off the ground while the bullfighters went in to distract the bull. Lucy turned to Jesse and gripped his arm. "Was that a good enough ride?" Just staying on wasn't enough in this kind of competition.

"That was one hell of a ride." Jesse sighed. "I'd say he's got it, but there's only one way to know for sure."

Jesse's eyes stayed fixed on the scoreboard, but Lucy watched Bowie as he jumped out of the arena with lithe grace and accepted a round of congratulatory pats on the back. Then his gaze also fixed on the scoreboard. As his numbers popped up, the crowd went wild.

"Did he win?" Maybe they were mad that he didn't score high enough. Lucy didn't know enough about the scoring to be sure.

"Yeah!!!" Jesse's deafening shout was all the answer she needed. "He did it."

Lucy clapped and cheered and whistled, as Bowie smiled at the crowds and doffed his hat.

Staff hurried to put an award podium into place in the arena, and Bowie and the other contestants—now ranked by final score—filed out to collect their prizes.

As she watched him accept the huge bronze trophy, and hold it high above his head, her joy and relief turned to doubt and anxiety.

Would he even want to talk to her? He'd said he wanted her here, but maybe that was just so he could prove to her that he was the best, despite her doubts about his character. Or perhaps he was simply being polite, since she flew all the way here to watch him.

On the other hand, he'd risked this title—and the glory and million-dollar prize—to fly back to Austin and try to uncover the conspiracy against him. In her selfish heart she couldn't help believing that he did that for her.

"Let's go down and meet him. He'll never make it back up here with all his fans flocking around him."

Lucy tried not to be jealous of the bling-studded cowgirls who flocked around Bowie, thrusting out things—including their tight-fitting T-shirts—for him to sign. Being short she couldn't even see Bowie once they got down on the floor, and she was glad Jesse took her hand to tug her through the crowds.

Her heart jumped against her rib cage as they drew close and she saw the brim of his hat, pushed back slightly.

"Lucy," his deep voice cut through the murmur of the crowd, and he strode between two people so they were face-to-face.

"Congratulations." She held her breath.

"I've made a decision." His serious expression caught her off guard. Her heart beat even faster.

"What?" A hush fell over the crowd.

"That was my last ride as a professional bull rider. I'm ready to head in a new direction."

An explosion of protest erupted from those around him. Bowie held up his hand. "Hey, I've had a great run and I've had my fun, but I have more important things to worry about now." He took Lucy's hands. "We're about to have a baby. That's a big commitment that I take very seriously. I don't want to be on the road, or risking my neck for no good reason, while Lucy's at home taking care of our child."

Did this mean that he intended for them to live together? Lucy was speechless with shock. She'd barely dared to dream that they could live together as a couple.

"And I have a ranch to run. I've neglected it all this time while I've been chasing the biggest, brightest buckle, but it's time for me to take that responsibility seriously, too."

Lucy's brain scrambled to make sense of his words. Bowie planned to settle down. Maybe not with her…but right next to her. That could work.

She tried to ignore the disappointment gathering in her chest. As long as he was in their child's life, that was all she cared about. She'd come this far in life without a man at her side, and she'd be just fine without one now.

"I'll be back, though," he continued. "Because I plan to breed the biggest, meanest, fastest, craziest bulls in the entire world."

A roar of chatter broke out, and Lucy was too dazed to focus on any one speaker. People peppered Bowie with questions about his plans and berated him for quitting the circuit when he was in a position to get great sponsors and bring more publicity to the sport.

He withstood the onslaught graciously, signing autographs all the while, until finally he looked up at then. "I hope you'll all excuse me, but I have a pressing engagement."

Amid protests, he took Lucy's arm and led her to the exit. They practically had to battle their way out and Lucy didn't even discover that Jesse was behind them, riding herd, until they exited the arena into the blazing afternoon son.

"That was a close one, bro." Jesse slapped Bowie on the back. "I almost thought they'd rather see you dead than retired."

"They're just surprised." Bowie squeezed Lucy. "I was a little surprised myself the first time the idea occurred to me. These things take some getting used to."

"You're going to love ranching."

"So you keep telling me. At least I'll have both of you to show me how it's done. Let's get out of here."

Lucy grabbed his arm. "Isn't there some big prize ceremony you have to attend?"

"Oh, yeah." Bowie frowned. "That. I won't let them down." He looked at Lucy, expression serious under his broad hat brim. "But I want some time alone with you, first."

Lucy felt a smile begin to creep across her face.

"If you'll let me, that is."

She nodded, too choked up to speak. Then she cleared her throat. "I'm so sorry I doubted you. I don't know what I was thinking."

"You were being sensible. Our child will need at least one sensible parent." He put his hands around her waist, straddling her belly. "I'm glad you pushed me to clear my name."

"Have they dropped the charges against you?" asked Jesse.

"Not yet. But that's going to be my number two focus going forward."

"What's number one?" asked Jesse.

"Number one—" He kissed Lucy softly on the lips. Heat flashed through her. She'd craved his kiss so much. "Is what I'm going to do to make this beautiful woman the happiest person on earth."

Lucy blinked, smile still creeping across her face. "That's a big goal."

"I don't do things by halves."

"He ain't lying," said Jesse. "And I think that's my cue to leave. I'll catch you all later for the awards ceremony." He tipped his hat to Lucy and strode off before either of them could protest.

"Your brother is pretty awesome," said Lucy, as he disappeared into the crowds. "Why doesn't he have a wife or girlfriend?"

Bowie shrugged. "Some girl broke his heart. I'm sure he'll get over it sooner or later. But that's his problem. My problem is what I'm going to do with you right now."

Her belly shivered, probably because the hungry look in his eyes gave her all kinds of ideas about the things he could do. "I think we should go back to your hotel," she whispered.

"I like the way you think. And it'll take an age to get our cars out of the crowded lot, so I'm going to run away with you."

Before she could grasp his meaning, he'd slid one arm under her butt and whisked her up in the air. Then he started jogging down the street, carrying her like he'd just rescued her from a burning building. Not surprisingly, people turned and stared.

"What are you doing?" She tried to protest, laughing and kicking her cowboy boots enough to rock him.

"It's an emergency situation."

"How?"

"If I don't make love to you in the next seven

minutes, I might bust into flames."

"I see. That does sound urgent." Flames were licking away in several different parts of her own body. "Maybe you should run faster."

24

Their lovemaking had an air of fevered desperation. At the awards ceremony afterward, they both kept collapsing into giggles, drunk on a chemical cocktail of passion. All night long people tried to convince Bowie to stay on the circuit for another year—"Win two championships and show your brother how it's done," etc.

But he stood firm. And he kept his arm around Lucy while he did it.

The next day they flew back to Austin separately. She invited him to stay at her ranch, but he told her he had business to attend to and he'd come as soon as he could.

Which was weird.

Back at High Pastures Ranch, the clients, the horses and Val were excited to see her. "See, aren't you glad I forced you to go?"

"You were right." Lucy and Val stood alone in the tack room, oiling bridles hanging from the tack hooks on the wall.

"He'd never have won without you there to support him."

"He most definitely would have. Still, it was fun, except for the part where I suddenly believed some strange woman's word over his. I guess I'm lucky he forgave me for that."

"He knows you're a relationship virgin."

Lucy shoved her. "You're so mean."

"Well, it's true. Learning to trust someone takes time. Especially someone as hot and famous as Bowie West."

"I hope watching my dad cheat on my mom hasn't caused a mutation in my DNA that causes me to jump to conclusions at every turn."

"Anyone would be skittish after that, but you'll be fine. Just give him the benefit of the doubt. Where is he, anyway?"

"He said he had business to attend to. Probably moving his millions around, including the fresh million he won in Vegas."

"Hard work but someone's got to do it. What's his plan for the ranch?"

"He wants to breed bucking bulls."

"That's awesome. You can combine your properties and expand your barn. Just think what you could do with a hundred acres of pasture." She put down her tack sponge and sighed.

"Val! He hasn't asked me to marry him."

"He'd better." Then Val frowned. "What would you say if he did?"

Lucy hesitated. "I do love him, but I don't want to rush into anything."

"Are you nuts? If you don't snatch him up, someone else will."

"We're already having a baby. That ties us together enough. I don't need a ring on my finger."

"Wait." Val froze and stared at her ring finger. "You're not wearing a ring on that finger. You usually do. I told you what bad luck that is—like a talisman to ward off men. I guess you finally listened to me."

Lucy looked at her empty finger with its white stripe where the ring had kept sun from her skin. She did usually wear a silver ring with horses running around it there. It became a habit during her long-distance relationship—to indicate that she was unavailable—and taking it off seemed like an admission of failure after they broke up. "I lost it in Vegas. I don't know how. I haven't taken it off in months but maybe it fell off in the shower." She and Bowie had made very hot, steamy and distracting love in that shower.

"Well, it's a good thing. A sign that you're ready to put a new ring on it."

"Which I'm not."

"Yet." Val winked at her and kept polishing.

Bowie showed up the next day armed with a bouquet of daisies and a stack of large coffee table books. Lucy took the daisies with a smile, then frowned as he carried the books into her house and heaved them onto the table.

Historic Houses of Texas was the one on top. She lifted it to reveal *Texas Modern,* with a picture of a glass-and-steel box surrounded by pinyon trees. "What are those for?"

"I don't get a kiss?" Bowie lifted a brow. His steady green gaze made her weak in the knees. The kiss only worsened the problem. The daisies didn't even make it into water. Soon they were upstairs knocking boots—literally—because they didn't want to waste time to get undressed.

They spend the rest of the day outside with the

horses, and he helped her mend a section of fence that had started to wobble. He excused himself and she headed out to ride one of her newer horses, a pretty palomino mare that showed promise as a forgiving lesson horse.

She heard Bowie's boots approach across the hard dirt of the stableyard. "Lucy."

"Hey, Bowie." Was he going to distract her again? He was hard to resist. She kept her eyes focused on her horse. "How's it going?"

"Great." He paused. She could feel his sexy green eyes burning into her back. "I have something to ask you."

"What's that?" She continued with long brushstrokes over her horse's back

His boot heel thunked on the concrete as he stepped toward her. "Lucy…" An odd tone in his voice made her finally turn. His face held a strange expression, intense and almost dazed. "I love you."

Emotion rushed through her, partly from his words and partly from the heartfelt way he said them. He'd never said it before. Did he really mean it, or was he just saying it because he thought she expected or needed it? "You love me? I bet you say that to all the girls." She tried to sound breezy and carefree. Which wasn't all that easy when you were carrying the guy's baby.

"I've never said it in my life before." She watched his Adam's apple move and heard the sincerity in his voice. Why was he suddenly so serious?

"And I've never said this, either." She watched, pulse quickening, as he reached into the back pocket of his jeans. He pulled out a small black box with gold tooling and opened it to reveal a sparkling ring.

Lucy blinked, hardly able to believe her eyes. "Lucy, will you marry me?"

Marry him? They'd only known each other a few weeks.

Yes, she was carrying his baby but that didn't mean...was he just asking her because he felt obliged to? She didn't have a daddy holding a shotgun, but maybe he felt it was the right thing to do.

Maybe it was the right thing to do?

Marriage was a lifetime commitment and one she took very seriously. Her heart pounded so hard he could probably hear it. She didn't dare look up at him so she kept her eyes focused on the ring, which glittered accusingly.

A lifetime with Bowie was sure to be an amazing adventure.

If it worked out. He did have a playboy reputation and she'd seen the kind of temptations that threw themselves at him on a daily basis.

On the other hand he'd risked missing the biggest competition of the year and his world title just to prove to her that he hadn't been unfaithful. That was worth something, right?

And she did love him. So much it hurt. So much that she'd been afraid to truly admit it to herself.

She finally dared to look up and meet his gaze, where worry danced in his beautiful jade eyes. "I love you, too." She said the words so quietly, they were barely a whisper. Conviction roared through her, and anticipation of a lifetime spent with the most exciting man she'd ever met. "And yes, I will marry you."

Breath rushed out of Bowie and relief swept over his expressive face. He plucked the ring from the box and slid it gently onto her bare ring finger. It fit like it was made just for her. That must be a sign of some kind.

"I wasn't sure you were going to say yes." His rueful grin made her smile.

"I wasn't sure I would either. You're a lot of man to handle." Joy rushed through her.

He looked a little sheepish. "I'm well broke. I just need finishing."

"I've got my hands full with half-broke horses." She shrugged, grin spreading across her mouth. "So what's one more challenge?"

He slid his arms around her waist and pulled her close. "I can't wait to spend the rest of my life with you."

"Impatient, aren't you?" she teased.

"Okay, maybe I can wait." He sighed. "I'll try to take life eight seconds at a time. Starting right—"

"Now." She interrupted him and kissed him hard on the mouth, teasing his tongue with hers and prolonging the kiss until they could both barely breathe. Exhilaration and excitement tingled in every inch of her body and she could almost swear she felt their baby moving in between them, even though she knew it was too early for that.

Then she pulled back. "And don't fall off, cowboy."

25

*S*pring

The days and nights were getting warmer and the sunsets later. The chores were done, and the horses—and bulls—settled for the night with their hay. The sun was still hovering above the horizon as Bowie and Lucy climbed up to the high pastures together—the ones she'd always seen from her ranch, that were actually on his. Now they were linked together as they were meant to be all along. "High Pastures is finally living up to its name," she said with a sigh.

"I'm glad we kept your name. I like it a lot better than Bitterroot Ranch."

Lucy nodded. "Is the tenant still asking if he can come back?"

"I thought we'd never get rid of him. He should count himself lucky he got a bargain for all those years." Bowie frowned. He'd been a crony of the West ranch foreman, who still hadn't been formally charged with anything. At least the DA's office had finally dropped the charges against Bowie, citing lack of evidence. He still planned to find the murderer, but planning their home, enjoying his new family, and taking care of their animals had taken precedence for now.

Bowie had brought his bulls from Jesse's and settled them into a newly constructed breeding and training facility. They'd soon be breaking ground on a new farmhouse-style home with a wraparound porch that would give them a view in all directions—over Lucy's newly expanded paddocks, the shimmering lake, the wooded hills and fields that would soon be carpeted with bluebonnets.

As usual Bowie found that he ended the day with a reassuring sense of satisfaction, the kind he used to feel after winning a race. The ranch was a huge machine with many moving parts, most of them living and breathing and changing every day. It was an invigorating challenge to keep the machine well oiled and it was keeping him well oiled too.

And then there was Lucy. He'd never thought that one woman could be everything to him: friend, partner, nurturer, and mind-blowingly erotic lover.

They laid out a blanket under a spreading oak tree. The last rays of the sun washed the landscape with pink, picking out the new fencing that surrounded the lush pasture now grazed by Lucy's horses.

They laid out the plates and Bowie unpacked the round wicker steamers he'd filled with delicate handmade dim sum. They sipped sparkling juice and ate the tasty morsels dipped in sweet and savory sauces.

"I imagine that our baby will be born with a taste for exotic foods," said Lucy, popping the last of a shrimp roll into her mouth.

"I hope so. It's great having an appreciative audience to cook for."

"Well, I love your cooking, and since I hate to cook myself it's a luxury to be with someone who enjoys it."

"Another one of the many reasons why we're perfect for each other." Bowie leaned forward and kissed her gently on the cheek. The scent of her always drove him crazy, made him want to bury his face in her soft, warm skin. Made him want to pull off her clothes and love her.

The sky was getting darker and the evening chorus starting its mating call. They put the plates back in the basket, their hands and arms casually brushing against each other, sending sparks of electricity leaping between them that were almost visible in the night air.

Bowie pulled Lucy gently toward him and kissed her firmly on the mouth. Her full lips always seemed to taunt him with their sensuality. Even when they were just talking he found himself watching them, wanting to lick them, to kiss them, to push his tongue inside them.

He pushed her gently back onto the blanket and climbed over her. He unbuttoned her shirt and parted it to reveal her breasts. The pregnancy had made them bigger and rounder and Lucy was a little self-conscious about them, but Bowie thought they were perfect at whatever size. He unhooked the front closure of her bra and let them spill out into his hands.

He licked her nipples and traced circles around them with his tongue. Soon her breasts would belong to their baby, and he didn't begrudge it. He couldn't wait to be a father.

He slipped off her shirt and bra gently, and let his hands slide down to the glorious full belly that signaled the presence of their child.

Their child. He'd gone against his instincts to leave

Lucy untouched and safe. The worst had happened, and it had had led him on a strange and magical path that he would never have willingly taken, but that he could now see was the only road to happiness.

He unbuttoned her jeans and carefully slid them off over her shapely legs, easing off her boots then stopping to marvel at the sight of her body glowing in the soft light of the stars.

Bowie parted her legs and lowered his face between her warm thighs. He could feel Lucy's hands moving through his hair as he licked, very gently, with soft, teasing flicks of the tongue, until she was shuddering and gasping with desire.

He traced a line of delicate kisses over the quivering skin of her belly, in between her smooth breasts, and up to her face. As his tongue slipped between her lips he entered her, a homecoming that never lost its thrill.

He heard her moan, uninhibited, as he pushed deeper inside her and she opened up for him. He relished the feel of their skin touching, their bodies sliding over each other, their scents mingling as they moved together.

I love you so much, Lucy, he thought. And then he said it, "I love you."

"I love you," she said softly, catching her breath as he thrust deeper inside her, pressing her buttons and driving her to the brink of ecstasy.

He loved to look at her face in the moment before she plunged over the edge and into the abyss of orgasm. Her dark-lashed eyes closed, her lips parted, sweet sounds escaping them as she urged him onward pulling him with her on a journey to the stars. He closed his eyes and lost himself in the surging tide that he could no longer swim against.

Crashing, groaning, he fell with her into the deep well of passion. Their bodies throbbed, shook and shivered together as they dove into that other realm that only lovers share, a warm lagoon of peace and ultimate intimacy.

"I'm glad I get to share my life with you," he breathed. "All the time I was running around, jumping on bulls and looking for excitement, I had no idea that was just an adrenaline rush. Happiness is something else altogether."

"Something I was too scared to reach for." Lucy's dark hair rested on his shoulder. "I thought intimacy and real love were for other people. After my last so-called boyfriend I didn't think I'd ever trust anyone again. But you made me feel again, and you proved to me that falling in love is worth the risk."

"And I intend to prove it to you for the rest of my life." He laid a soft kiss on her cheek.

Lucy stroked his tangled hair. "I know you're a man of your word and you don't back down from a challenge."

He grinned. "So hang on tight for the ride of your life."

THE END

Next in the **Hearts of the West** series:

His Untamed Heart:
The Cowboy's Christmas Reunion

Tara Kent is reeling from a broken engagement and the collapse of her business. The last person she wants to see is Jesse West, the rich cowboy who seduced her for revenge sex two years earlier. Unfortunately, designing his guest villas would save her from financial disaster.

Revenge was the furthest thing from Jesse's mind when he finally made love to the woman of his dreams, but after the way Lily's treated him since, he'll take what he can get. Opposites attract and soon Jesse finds himself planning a happy ever after. He's known for winning over the most ornery horses, but winning Lily's heart is proving to be far more of a challenge.

Tara's falling hard for the rugged and capable horse trainer, but she knows she can't give him what he wants most, so she tries her best to keep her heart—and her dreams—under wraps.

Join the new release newsletter at
www.jenlewis.com.

ABOUT THE AUTHOR

Jennifer Lewis loves heat in all its forms including spicy food, steamy temperatures and smoking hot heroes. She is a USA TODAY bestselling author and her books have been translated into more than twenty languages. She lives in sunny South Florida and when she's not sitting at her laptop she can often be found at the beach. Read more about her books and join her new release mailing list at www.jenlewis.com.

www.ingramcontent.com/pod-product-compliance
Lightning Source LLC
Chambersburg PA
CBHW022009170626
46808CB00001B/335